Branded Words

*Branded Words is a collection of the best writings
published by the online magazine Short Story Library
during the year 2009.*

Written By:

Angel Zapata
Bob Burnett
Anne Brooke
Bill Charles
Brad M. Bucklin
Caroline Burman
E.K. Entrada
Elaine Medline
Grant J. Bergland
Heather Grange
Holly Day
Ian Lamberto
James Bowler
James Cotter
John Ammirati
John Bruce
John Grey
John Wiswell
John Yamrus
Jordan Eudy
Leigh Byrne
Len Joy
Michael McLaughlin
Patricia McCowan
RD Armstrong
Richard Grossman
Ryan Sayles
Sarah R. Larson
T. Paul Buzan

This is a work of fiction. Names, characters, and events are works of the author's imagination. Any resemblance to actual names or events is purely coincidental.

Edited by Casey Quinn

ISBN: 978-0-9822434-5-9

Published by:
ReadMe Publishing
http://readme.us.com

Contents

Short Stories

Casualties

By Len Joy

The waitress refills my coffee. It's five after eight and Karen is late as usual. From my table at Windows on the 107th floor, I have an awesome view of New York harbor. The September sky is so clear and blue it doesn't look real. It's a heartbreaking blue. The vessels in the harbor look like toy boats. I follow one of them as it turns east towards the ocean. I imagine myself at the wheel, salt spray in my face, racing into the morning sun. Heading nowhere. Happy.

I made seven million dollars last year. I have a wife who's take-your-breath-away beautiful and my daughter Cassie, well, she's the best. I live in a fifteen room mansion in New Hartford. That's about ten rooms more than Karen and I need. We have a tennis court I never use, a swimming pool and a carriage house.

I'm forty seven years old and I've only loved one woman in my life.

***

The bulletin board at the back of Willard Straight Hall was plastered with political posters. There were a dozen supporting McGovern and almost as many for the Socialist candidate. There was only one Nixon poster that had survived, and someone had given the President a Hitler-like mustache. It didn't appear that Nixon was going to carry Cornell.

This was supposed to be an orientation mixer for the Class of 1976, but it appeared that everyone but me had already mixed. I wandered through the hall trying not to look like some hick from a town with one traffic light, and ended up staring at the President.

I had decided that Nixon actually looked better with the mustache when a girl with tangled brown hair, her boobs bouncing free under her red Cornell Frosh tee-shirt, walked over to me. She stared at my nametag.

"So Colin O'Keefe, do you think we should re-elect a President who can't even organize a third-rate burglary?" Before I could answer she took hold of my nametag so she could read the address line below the name. "Where the hell is Clyde Falls?"

I tried to look surprised. "You've never heard of the Wayne County Onion Festival?"

She wrinkled her nose. "You celebrate onions?"

"Actually the festival's in Elba. But Clyde Falls is just down the road on Highway K," I said. I wanted to return the favor and grab her nametag, but she had pasted it just above her left nipple and I didn't have the guts. I could tell from her accent that she was a New Yorker. Cornell was full of them. "Where the hell's Brooklyn, Maria Pasquale?"

"That's Pa-squal-e'. Three syllables. Remember the name. One day there will be a wing in MOMA for my work," she said, jabbing me in the chest.

"Moma?"

She rolled her eyes. "How about another beer, farm boy?"

***

Maria was not one to be tied down by her possessions. Her apartment, a small studio at the bottom of one those ridiculous steep hills that surrounded the campus, was cluttered, but nearly unfurnished. She had a mattress with a comforter in the middle of the floor, a dresser in one corner and a small desk and lamp in another. The air was thick with the smell of paint and turpentine. Sketchpads, brushes, canvases and tubes of paint covered the floor and the mattress.

She turned on the lamp, which cast a soft amber glow over the small room. She plowed the art supplies off the mattress and threw herself facedown on the bed. She patted the mattress. "Come here, Colin. I promise not to bite. Tell me what it was like to grow up in Mayberry."

I had never been in a girl's bedroom before. Back home we'd make out in our cars at the drive-in movies, or if the girl was easy, on one of the back roads, but I never got to see their bedroom. I doubted they looked like Maria's room. I flopped down next to her.

"So what do you want to know? My dad's a dairy farmer. We got about a hundred Holsteins, half dozen Jerseys, couple of Guernseys."

"Cows? You have to milk them every day?"

"I guess you don't have many cows in Brooklyn. What do your parents do?"

Maria flipped over and stared up at the ceiling. "My dad was a cop. He died when I was sixteen. My mother ran off when I was two. Dad always said she was a free spirit." Maria made imaginary quote marks as she spit out the words.

"I'm sorry."

"Don't be." She rolled on to her side and rested her hand on my chest. "I'll bet you had plenty of girlfriends. Probably even got to date a cheerleader," she said. She said cheerleader like it was royalty, or some mysterious species.

"You weren't a cheerleader?"

Maria sat up and cupped her boobs. "What? You don't think a voluptuous Italian chick can shake her tits and ass as good as some long-legged dairy queen Barbie?"

I squeezed her ass as I pulled her on top of me. "I don't know. Maybe."

She nuzzled my neck. "So tell me. What's it like to kiss a cheerleader?"

"Don't you know?" I asked.

She looked at me and laughed. "Good one, farm-boy. You get a point for that."

Before she could come up with another question I kissed her. "It's not as good as kissing an artist," I said.

She grabbed my shoulders and rolled us over so she was on top. She pulled off her tee-shirt and threw it on the floor. "I'll bet you didn't know any girls like me in Clyde Falls."

***

Two weeks after Nixon ran the table on hapless George McGovern I moved into Maria's place. I was unpacking my stuff, trying to squeeze it into the small dresser Maria provided, when I found a framed photograph of little Maria, wearing a Yankees cap, sitting on her father's lap. He was decked out in his NYPD dress uniform.

"Don't tell me you're a Yankee fan," I said.

Maria took the frame and dusted it off with her tee-shirt. "I was looking for this." She placed it on the bookshelf next to the alarm clock. She sat down on the bed, her hands in her lap, as she stared at the faded photo. "My Dad loved the Yankees. He would have traded me for one more World Series."

I put my arm around her. "No." I shook my head. "Not for ten World Series."

***

We spent the Christmas break with my parents in Clyde Falls. At school Maria hardly took the time to eat, but as soon as she got to Clyde Falls, she acted like she lived in the kitchen. Helped my mother with every meal and she got along great with my father. Maria loved to ask questions and Dad loved to talk. By the end of our stay she probably could have passed the mid-terms in the Ag school. She even got up one morning at four a.m. so she could watch him and his crew do the milking.

The two weeks flew by. On our last day we hiked up to the ridge that overlooked our farmhouse.

"How could you live here all your life and not want to paint this scene?" Maria asked.

"The sun, the snow. Look how the light filters through the trees of the orchard, and that stream, sorry, I mean crick. It's so goddamn alive." She sketched for an hour and would have stayed longer, if I hadn't convinced her that frostbitten fingers would not be good for her career.

The next day, when we were driving back to Cornell, she asked, "Do you think your parents like me?"

I looked over at her to see if she was joking. "Well my mom thinks you ought to wear a bra, but Dad's fine with your tits flopping around."

She punched me in the shoulder. "I'm serious. They're so nice. I want them to like me." She rubbed my shoulder. "Sorry."

"Do you think my mother would give you her special recipe for tuna casserole if she didn't think you were worthy?"

She sat back to consider the possibility. "I guess not," she said slowly. "And I promise to never make it. What about your father?"

I had to laugh. "Are you kidding? You're an artist. He worships the ground you walk on."

I grabbed her hand before she could punch me again. "You think my father's Old McDonald, but he's a renaissance man. He made me take piano lessons, violin. One summer he had my mother drive me to Rochester to take ballet classes. I lived in mortal fear my buddies would find out."

"So where's your violin."

"After listening to me practice for six excruciating months he finally conceded I had no talent."

Maria slid over next to me and put her hand in my crotch. "Not true. You're a very talented lover."

***

Maria was talented. I knew that because at every party we went to one of her artist-friends would tell me. This news was usually delivered to me as though I were some sort of Neanderthal who had stumbled upon a precious artifact and had no idea of its value. I think they were afraid I might break her or something.

In the spring of our junior year Maria had a major exhibition at a new gallery off-campus. It was nearly two a.m. by the time we made it back to our apartment after the opening.

"Should we open a bottle of champagne to celebrate?" I teased. Maria was splayed on the bed, her arm covering her eyes. She had stripped off her black cocktail dress and was naked except for her bikini panties.

"My god, I can't take all this being nice shit. My jaw hurts from smiling. Turn off the light and come here farm boy."

I sat on the edge of the bed and untied my dress shoes. "Who was that skinny black dude?"

"You mean Baldwin? He teaches oil painting. Why?"

"He told me you should have applied for that fellowship in Florence. What was he talking about?"

Maria made a dismissive pffft sound. "He's out of his mind. I don't have a chance of getting into that program."

"Why not? You're really good, M. Everyone says so."

"It's three years. I'd have to start in the fall. I can't do that."

Baldwin had told me the fellowship was a once in a lifetime chance that could make her career. At that moment, as I sat there on the edge of her bed taking off my clunky wing-tips, I had what her artist friends would probably call an epiphany. It wasn't a blinding flash of light or anything like that, it was more like a switch clicked on in my brain and I knew, without any doubt, that Maria had to apply for that fellowship.

"Why don't you go for it?" I asked.

She ignored me, scooted over to where I was sitting, and pressed her bare breasts into my back. "Come on Colin, don't you want to show me how talented you are?"

"Baldwin said you still had time."

She shoved me away and folded her arms. "It's a waste of time. Besides the Yankees just signed Catfish Hunter. I think we can win the series this year."

"I bet you'll get in."

She stood up. "For christsake, Salomon Gutierrez is in that program. And Meulier. Fucking Anton Meulier. I'm not in their league." She jumped off the bed and skipped over to the sink to brush her teeth.

"If you don't apply I'm going to tell my father you don't think you're good enough."

Maria stared at me in mock horror. "Oh god, don't do that. He'll give me that lecture about reaching for the stars." She turned off the light and jumped back on the bed next to me, her head buried in the pillow. "Do you really think I should?"

"What do you have to lose?"

***

Most of us have a day that we remember all our lives. I don't mean those landmarks like Pearl Harbor or Kennedy's assassination. I mean a day that changes the course of our life. The day that we take the road less traveled and it really does make all the difference. May 15, 1975 was my day.

Classes were over for the year and final grades had been posted. I was headed back to the apartment to tell Maria I'd aced my International Econ final. When I opened the door I found her staring out the window, clutching a letter. She looked at me. There were tears in her eyes, but she was smiling.

"I got in," she said, handing me the letter.

I stared at the paper. I could see the words, but I couldn't read them. I took a deep breath.

"That's fantastic." I really tried to smile, but I couldn't make my face work right. It felt rubbery, numb.

"Come with me, Colin. Senior year abroad. It'll be great. Your Dad will be ecstatic."

I wrapped my arms around her, the letter still clutched in my hand. My legs trembled.

"Will you marry me, Maria?" I had fantasized about asking her that question ever since the day we met, but this wasn't how I imagined it. She thought I was joking, but after she looked at me for a moment her expression softened. She didn't want to hurt me.

"We don't need some silly ceremony," she said.

"I need it. I'll never find someone I love more than you. I want to be the husband of Maria Pasquale. I can take care of you. Clean your paintbrushes. Remind you to eat. But I need to be your husband. I can't just be your boyfriend."

"You aren't just my boyfriend," she said, her voice breaking.

I loosened my grip on her and the letter slipped from my hand. "I'm sorry. I don't want to ruin your day. We should be celebrating."

"Colin, I love you. Please come with me." She squeezed my hand so hard it hurt.

"I will M. I promise. After graduation. It's only a year. That will give you time to get settled in." I kissed away her tears. "Maria you are going to be the toast of Florence."

On that day I was certain I had made the right choice. I was all caught up in the romantic bullshit that somehow I was setting her free. I wish I had a do-over because I'd follow her to Hell and back if I had another chance.

I knew she would thrive in Florence. And I knew that her new world, like an inferno, would consume our relationship. I knew we would never survive the separation.

I was right.

She left for Europe in July and in December she wrote to tell me that she had moved in with Anton Meulier.

Fucking Anton Meulier.

***

A week before Thanksgiving, four weeks before I got Maria's Anton Meulier letter, my buddies insisted I come with them to a party at the Deke house. The band was literally deafening, and the place was packed with sweaty fraternity guys and their dates. It took me ten minutes just to make my way to the front of the bar. Drink in hand, I wheeled around and ran right into the most beautiful girl I had ever seen. I spilled my drink on her.

"I'm sorry," I said.

She laughed. "It's okay I'm used to it. Back in New Hartford the boys were always falling over themselves to bring me a drink."

Karen was truly stunning. She had blonde hair and pale blue eyes and was wearing a very short black mini-dress that showed off her long tanned legs. I bought her a drink and we went outside where we could talk.

She was a freshman, majoring in English. It was easy to talk to her. She was friendly and uncomplicated. When I walked her back to the dorm, I thought about kissing her, but I didn't.

I ran into her again just before Christmas break, right after I got the letter from Maria. We shared a pitcher of beer at the Campus Inn. Karen asked if she could see my apartment.

We made love on Maria's old bed.

***

Sometimes we determine the course of our lives by the actions we take and sometimes we just go along for the ride, like a leaf in a stream. I chose not to follow Maria to Florence. A decision I came to regret, but at least a decision I made. With Karen, I just jumped in the river and let the current take me.

In April I was accepted at Yale Law School. Two weeks later Karen told me she was pregnant. I asked her if she wanted to get married. It was more a question than a proposal, but she said yes. Then she started crying and told me how happy we were going to be.

We were married in June, ten days after I graduated. I gave up on law school and went to work for Karen's father.

***

It wasn't as though I woke up every day thinking about Maria. I wasn't obsessed. Karen was a good person. We were compatible. And Cassie, our daughter, was a beautiful diversion. Maybe I wasn't the happiest guy on the block, but I wasn't a bad husband. By the time Cassie graduated from NYU and took an advertising job in San Francisco, sometimes months would pass without me even thinking about Maria.

Then last year on New Year's Day, Karen dragged me to a new gallery in SoHo. I was hung over from the firm's big Millennium party and I had wandered into the back room of the gallery, looking for a restroom, when I saw the painting. I was staring at it, not believing my eyes, when the owner of the gallery walked up to me. She was rail-thin with dyed black hair, and was smoking a cigarette.

"Have you ever seen anything like that? Such emotion. And sadness." She had a nasally, Bronx accent.

"Where did you get it?"

"Barcelona. On the Rambla. An American. She was selling everything, moving to the north coast with her boyfriend. Can you believe it? I bought it for a hundred dollars. Of course she didn't want to sell." She raised her chin to blow her smoke towards the lofted ceiling.

"Didn't want to sell?"

"Apparently it had sentimental value. She had a big argument with her boyfriend. I didn't want to get in the middle of that scene so I told her I'd changed my mind. But that evening he brought it to my hotel." She shrugged her shoulders and turned up her palms. "What could I do?"

"Who's the artist?" I asked, peering at the canvas.

"Don't know. She just signed it, 'M.' I think it's a scene from northern Italy."

The smoke from her cigarette was burning my eyes and it was difficult to breathe. I thought my heart was going to pound through my chest. "No," I whispered, shaking my head, "it's not Italy. Excuse me, I need some air."

I turned my back on Maria's painting of the farmhouse in Clyde Falls on a gloomy, foreboding autumn day. I raced out of the gallery before anyone could see that I was crying.

***

Up until that day, I was doing okay. Things were in balance. My life wasn't perfect, but whose is? I was making it work, but that goddamn painting was like the pebble that unleashes a landslide.

I had to find Maria. I went back to the gallery owner the next day and she gave me the name of a friend who worked for a major gallery in Barcelona. I called her that night. She didn't know Maria but she gave me a list of smaller dealers that might have run into her. I started calling. I followed every lead. Finally, after three months, I found an art dealer who had purchased one of her paintings and thought she was living outside San Sebastian. He said she usually came south to Barcelona in the fall.

I sent him a five thousand dollar deposit for her next painting, and promised another five if he'd contact me as soon as she made an appearance. He thought I was a crazy American, but last week he called me. Maria's boyfriend was bringing him three of her paintings. He was going to meet with him this Saturday, the 15th. I made a reservation to fly to Barcelona on Friday.

***

The boat I'm watching heads out to sea and disappears as the waitress approaches my table again. "More coffee, Mr. O'Keefe? Will you be having breakfast?"

"Please," I say, moving the cup to my left side. "I'll wait to order. My wife's joining me."

"Very good, sir. Beautiful morning, isn't it?"

I look at my watch. Eight ten. I take a deep breath and exhale slowly. Usually when Karen comes into the city we meet at the end of the day for dinner, but today she had wanted to meet for breakfast at Windows. Married twenty-five years and she still didn't understand that this is a damn inconvenient time for me to get away. My day begins at five and by eight the London markets are in their final hour and New York's preparing to open.

From behind me I can hear Karen greeting the host. "Good morning, Maurice. It is a lovely day." Her voice is clear, mellifluous.

I turn and watch as she glides towards our table, looking self-possessed, entitled. Her blonde hair is cut stylishly short and her pale-blue halter dress matches her eyes.

"Hi honey, sorry I'm late," she brushes a kiss on my lips.

The host seats her to my left so we both have a view of the harbor. I hand her the menu.

"I don't have much time. I need to leave by eight forty-five."

She takes out her reading glasses and starts to flip through the pages. She always looks at every page and then orders the fruit plate.

"What are you going to have dear?"

"Eggs benedict."

She reaches over and gently brushes her fingers through my hair. "Look at you. Not a touch of grey and you can still eat whatever you want. I'll just have the fruit plate."

I give the waitress our order. "What have you planned for today?"

She smiles and clasps her hands. "I have a fabulous day planned. A facial and manicure at the Waldorf at ten. Lunch in Central Park, and then I'm going to check out a new boutique in the west Village. I'd like to see the Gorky exhibition at MOMA if I have time. Maybe you can meet me there after work?"

"I don't know. Depends how the day goes."

"Mother called as I was leaving."

Karen's mother is always calling. Those calls never bring good news.

"She said Father's retirement is driving her crazy. He wants to run their home like a business."

I try not to laugh. "Has he come up with a mission statement yet? Given your mom some measurable objectives. Told her how people don't plan to fail, they fail to plan."

"Stop it, Colin. This is hard for Mom."

"I had an email from Cassie. She likes her new job."

Karen puts down her coffee and grabs my hand. "Do you think you could take a week off so we could visit her? The Bay area is so beautiful in the fall."

The servers arrive with our orders. It's eight twenty-five. I slice the eggs benedict into bite-size pieces.

Karen, holding a forkful of honeydew in one hand, reaches over and grabs my wrist. "Slow down, dear. You don't have to race out and milk the cows."

I pull my hand a way and look at my watch. It's eight twenty-eight.

"Can you get away for a week?" she asks again.

"I don't know. I'll have to check my schedule."

Karen pulls back in her chair. Now she's annoyed. "Of course you do," she says with a slight shake of her head. She extracts a leather-bound planner from her purse. "Tomorrow we have concert tickets, and on Friday, the fourteenth, we have your reunion reception at the Midtown Club. A chance to see all your old Cornell classmates."

I finish the eggs and throw my napkin on the plate. "I don't want to go to that."

"But it's the twenty-fifth reunion – there should be some fresh faces – it's a milestone."

I sign the check and stand up to go. "There's nobody I want to see. Look I have to leave now. You stay. Enjoy your coffee, I'll check in with you later. Maybe we can do the Gorky thing."

"Oh, I almost forgot." Karen brings her hand up to cover her mouth. She starts searching through her bag. "I was reading the Cornell newsletter. Remember that girl you used to date? Marie? The artist?"

"What about her?" I sit back down.

"It was in the alumni section." She continues to sift through the contents of her bag. "Where is it? I know I brought it."

"Karen, just tell me what the goddamn thing said." My voice sounds strained.

Karen notices too. She looks at me, puzzled. "Well this actually happened a year ago. Can you believe it? You'd think Cornell could do a better job of keeping track of their alumni."

I start to reach for my coffee cup, but my hands are shaking.

"She died. In Paris. They didn't give details. You know, like they never do when someone commits suicide or dies from AIDS or a drug overdose. I am sorry, Colin. I know Marie was your friend."

I slump back in my chair.

"Maria," I whisper. "Her name was Maria. She was from Brooklyn."

It's eight forty-two.

***

Maria takes my hand as our boat races out to sea. The sun sparkles on the water and salt spray stings our faces. The sky is so blue it doesn't look real.

It is a heartbreaking blue.

Warren's Post

By Sarah R. Larson

"It's a warm one."

"You bet."

And that was it. The same old men spent their afternoons the summer of 1969 lollygagging in Patsy's Diner, drinking diluted lemonade and listening to the second-hand radio that squawked Buck Owens and his Kansas City Song. It was too hot to agree with the opinion and too hot to disagree. No one argued because beginning an argument took effort. No one moved because it would take the strength of Coach Paulson's varsity quarterback to peel the sweaty geezers off their seats.

I fidgeted in my small place at the far end of Patsy's counter. The room was so hot my skinny legs under my paisley-printed sundress stuck to the plastic seat of my favorite stool. The sweltering air clung to the outer rim of my water glass in rivers of condensation and someone's rebel cigarette smoke mixed with the sweet scent of boiling cabbage. I tried to ignore the biting flies. Many of them dove head-long into poisoned fly traps hanging in lethal ribbons around our heads. Patsy executed the rest with her purple, plastic fly swatter.

The temperature had reached a sweltering one hundred and three degrees, even in the shade, and dogs loitered outside under the diner's awning, staring pitifully through the open door and lapping at the air. As I sat in the diner, this summer of 1969, I listened sleepily to Forest County's oldest pair of veterans talk to their elderly neighbors about everything and Vietnam.

Grant and Harvard Lee, twins and as old as the fields, flew British Sopwith Camel aircraft for Great Britain in the First World War. The men never joined an air raid but delivered messages to allied France. Three times they miscalculated the distance and flew into Germany. Three times they came back to the island with their aircraft shredded to pieces and too stubborn to admit they'd gone the wrong way.

The Lees disgraced their squadron. They became heroes in our town. Anything stupid but accomplished made someone a hero in Forest County. Daily, at least one of them reserved the right to have his say about some political matter. But today, the heat had taken the conservatism right out of them. Today, the twins had nothing to talk about. With a communal sigh of relief, Patsy's patrons recited their prayers over their greasy breakfasts in blessed silence.

"It's a warm one," Harvard said again when the silence had been too long.

"You bet."

I thought this week's heat wave made Forest County hotter than hell.

I was twelve years old the summer of 1969. Every day I sat at the end of Patsy's counter spinning and kicking and twirling at my stool. I listened to the veterans argue their way through breakfast. I watched Patsy make the young men blush by sidling up to the counter with an aroma of My Sin Eau de Toilette clouding around her hairnet. She had a flair for flirting. My mother said she earned the extra tips she received from the lonely bachelor farmers. Sometimes, I imitated her techniques alone in my bedroom. Sometimes, when Patsy wasn't looking, I practiced on Jonny.

Jonny Koch was Patsy's hired help. He covered for Patsy when she took her breaks and he served the veterans their dessert. They tipped him well because Jonny was a patriot, though he hadn't been drafted yet. I tipped him too because I liked the songs he whistled. His voice was still changing and he whistled to cover it up. I loved him for it. I loved Jonny Koch but I didn't know why. His eyes bugged out and he moved too fast. It was as if he had something to prove but couldn't.

I had one friend in 1969-Alpa, a brown and lonely girl. She followed me like an inquisitive Indian shadow through every alley and vacant cul-de-sac in the neighborhood. She went with me to Lincoln High where I liked to watch the dusty construction of the new classroom building. She came with me to the E-Z Stop, where I sat by the ice chest and counted the pickup trucks with dented fenders. Sometimes Alpa followed me home where my parents didn't trust her.

Alpa went everywhere. She went everywhere but the diner. I told her I'd buy her a Coke if she came in. She said no. She didn't like old men. She didn't like Patsy. She thought the veterans knew too much and she figured Patsy didn't know anything at all to make up for it. No one in the diner trusted her anyway; she was visiting from the Reservation.

As I sat at Patsy's counter this boiling day in 1969, I turned my head to see Alpa standing outside the diner's large picture window. She'd been standing there for an hour, waiting with her nose up against the glass. She gazed irritably into the restaurant from her safe place on the sidewalk, while the neighborhood dogs circled her with whimpering sighs. Her expression talked to me and her brown legs shifted restlessly under her dress. Her nervous eyes shuttled back and forth between Patsy and the twins. When Jonny walked into the room, she turned and fell face-forward over her bicycle.

"The mouse is back," Johnny whispered to the dessert carousel.

I sighed. It was hot.

The stranger came into the diner at ten o'clock. He was a tall, slender man with a mustache and when he walked through the open door, he cast a slim, willowy shadow over the counter. He walked the length of the counter with Midwestern ease and settled himself on the stool closest to me. In respectful silence, he removed his weathered cap. It read "Minnesota Grain Pearling Company". Greasy stains rimmed the bill and the edges were frayed. His hair was long and flat and wet with the heat.

The man looked respectable otherwise. He wore a shirt with wide lapels and jeans, well-worn and faded. He was clean. I knew by looking at him that he was someone my father would've been friends with-the uncle type, slim and comfortable and modest. Something, though, made him different. He looked like the other men, casual and hardworking, but his face wasn't tired.

The stranger looked at me suddenly. Perspiration made his forehead shiny and streams of sweat ran into his gentle eyes. He didn't say anything but reached around me to grab a menu. He flipped it open and found the insides gone.

"She has her specials for the regulars," I told him. "You don't need a menu. She'll tell you what to get."

The stranger closed the menu. A subtle smile formed at the side of his mouth, as if he'd seen things and only wanted to laugh at our world. I'd seen things too, so I frowned at him. Anyway, I thought I'd seen things. There wasn't anything left to see in this part of the country, where the fields were tired of producing and the families were tired of getting by.

"Patsy, you got a costumer," Harvard announced.

Patsy ignored the veteran but eyed the visitor with interest. She patted her hairnet. Coyly, she helped Jonny set up the electrical fan he'd brought from home. The antique blades clicked and clattered until it finally whirred into motion. As soon as she could, Patsy assumed her duties and poured the man a glass of water.

"You from around here?"

"Just moved in."

"From where?"

"Duluth."

"Ah."

"My folks are there. My brother went to Vietnam."

"A patriot?" Harvard wanted to know.

"He was. Say, I need directions."

Bored with the conversation, I glanced at the picture window. Alpa was still there, itching the sides of her dress impatiently. She reached down to rub a scab on her knee and blood smeared from her fingertips. She knelt down to wipe the mess on the cement and one of her canine friends nudged her aside to look at it.

"Who're you looking for?" Harvard asked the stranger with smug authority. He pulled out his handkerchief and dried his upper lip.

"I'm looking for the Barclay place."

The room grew silent. The hot air seemed closer. Buck Owens stopped singing his Kansas City Song because the radio tower lost the signal again. It happened when the humidity was high.

At the same time, the whirring of the electrical fan stopped. It shorted, mid rotation, and Jonny stepped back in painful protest. Patsy pursed her lips to form a suspicious O and the twins swallowed over and over. They were unusually silent, though Grant moved slightly on his stool. The dry, tired gears complained under the weight of his seat.

"You know Scott Barclay?" Grant finally asked, his doughnut sitting half eaten in his sweaty palm.

"Got his mail," the stranger said.

The man waved a hand at the diner's picture window. We all saw the Ford Sedan, rusty and white and steamy hot in the un-shaded street. It was old, from the 1950s, and there was a faded place on the car's exterior where the Ford decal had been peeled away. Inside the car, sitting tall in the back seat, were trays of letters. A big flat box moved slightly but no one was there. I suddenly saw Alpa's brown Indian face appear on the other side of the vehicle. She watched the curious box through the window with interest.

"You're the new rural post," Harvard observed with suspicious curiosity.

The postman pulled his own handkerchief out of his pocket. He patted his high cheek bones with the damp piece of linen. Sweat ran down into his mouth. "I'm looking for the Barclay place."

Harvard nodded, a little harder. Everyone knew the Barclays. Scott Barclay had moved into Forest County over a year ago with his large, unusual family. He had twelve children. I'd seen the oldest seven walking to school across Henderson's field. They attended the last one-room schoolhouse in Forest County and the four oldest children, Allison, Brianna, Colleen, and Davin, taught their younger siblings. No one offered to teach there. The rest of the kids in Forest County attended the school in town, after the state issued the consolidation. The Barclays didn't go to public school. The Barclays were Catholic.

"Barclay, he came from the East," Jonny said, wistful. The veterans' critical eyes reprimanded their own patriot with a steely glance. Jonny swallowed his words. "I've only been as far as Wisconsin."

"Mother's pastor told me that the Barclays are building a memorial in their back yard," Patsy said, reaching over the counter with her lemonade jug. She refilled Grant's empty glass. Out of habit, she filled a new glass and set it down in front of the stranger. The postman stared reluctantly at the pale yellow liquid with no ice. He'd have to drink it now.

"They're building it for the president."

"The president?"

The postman sniffed the lemonade and reached for the doughnut jar.

"Kennedy?"

"A memorial," Patsy insisted, handing the man a napkin. "With an altar. That's why they go to church at home."

Patsy didn't say anything else. My mother had told me that the Barclays were the only Catholics in Forest County. Forest County didn't have any Catholic churches. According to the patriarchs, the county never would. But going to church at home, where no one could see you, was about as sacrilegious as starting your own Catholic school.

"I have their mail," the postman repeated. He braved a sip of his lemonade and his cheeks pinched comically.

"Makes sense," Jonny said.

Catholics wrote letters too. My mother had gotten a letter from a Catholic once.

"The Barclays are from the East," Harvard said, pretending Jonny had never pointed it out. "They're socialists."

"Change isn't always bad," the postman said.

Jonny fiddled with the fan.

"Something's wound too tight," Harvard interrupted, pointing at Jonny and his ancient contraption. "Something's wound up inside of it."

"It could go faster," Grant added.

Patsy gave the postman his silverware and wrote up a lunch order special. She gave her regulars the fried chicken. She gave the postman the meatloaf.

"You could fry an egg on the sidewalk in this heat," Patsy observed as she handed Jonny the order slip.

"You could fry an egg in a skillet," the stranger replied. "Oh, dagnabbit!"

The stranger suddenly tipped off his stool and ran for the door. I didn't miss the elaborate string of moderate profanity he created with his words. Harvard and Grant nearly fell off their stools. Patsy dropped her lemonade jug and almost repeated the postman's sentiments.

I ran to the window. I saw Alpa reach for her bike in a flurry of self-conscious panic as the postman ran swearing to his Sedan. She took off on her bike and rode as fast as she could down the street, in the direction of the Piggly Wiggly.

"That silly mouse," Jonny chuckled.

"She's from the Reservation," I reasoned.

In a matter of minutes, the postman had returned. He stood breathing with irritable disgust. He had the long box in his arms and dumped it unceremoniously onto the counter. I heard a flurry of chirping.

"Chicks," the postman explained. He fell on his stool again and ignored the patrons' stares. "Mail-order birds. The heat could kill 'em."

Pasty boldly removed the lid from the box as the postman dried his face with his handkerchief again.

"It's hotter than hell," he said.

I hurried from the window and climbed up to the counter to have myself a look. Jonny watched me first, and then followed me. The twins, slower and a bit more reluctant, couldn't help themselves. They wiggled their aging bodies into the group and stretched their necks to see.

"They can't breathe in there."

"Sure they can. Anyway, they won't be in there for long."

"Where'd they come from?"

"Catalogue."

"That one looks sick."

"That one's dead."

"Dagnabbit."

"I could water 'em."

"Get 'em some water, Patsy," Harvard commissioned.

And that was it. For the next hour and a half, the postman, who told us to call him Bick Warren, helped Jonny and Patsy revive the heat-inflicted chicks. The twins supervised and held the little birds in their clumsy, arthritic hands when told to do so. The old veterans pretended to mind. They chuckled, but then cleared their throats. They smiled, but then frowned, and said that it was too hot to hold anything with fluff. Harvard yelped when one of the babies peed on him and everybody laughed.

I watched. I petted. I looked at Jonny, and he looked at me when he nestled one of the sleeping chicks in my sweaty fingers. I held the bird to my flushed cheek while Jonny tried to cool our faces with an empty menu. His fan still wasn't working right.

The radio picked up the tower signal again. Buck Owens sang us a song while the veterans told Bick Warren about Germany and Sopwith Camel aircraft. I listened to the stories again but I heard them this time. Bick Warren liked the stories. His eyes grew distant when the twins turned the topic from Germany to our boys in Vietnam.

"Well, anyway," Harvard finally breathed, awkwardly dumping the last baby chick into the cardboard box. "Where are they off to?"

He meant the birds.

"The Barclays."

The room grew suddenly close again. I coughed, choking on the hot air that didn't move. Patsy gave me a glass of water.

"These are Scott Barclay's birds?" Grant hesitated, eyeing the box. He slowly reached for the lid and slid it into place. The chirps and the peeps and the scratches were muffled now. I missed the sound.

The room was quiet. The room was quiet for too long.

"Well," Patsy breathed, wiping her fingers slowly on a towel. Harvard stared at his fingers, rubbing them as if he wasn't sure he should clean them too.

Grant took a drink of lemonade. Bick Warren stood to leave. The postman rubbed his high forehead with the back of his hand and slipped the Minnesota Grain Pearling Company cap back over his hair.

"See you folks."

The man grabbed the box a little too hard. I heard the gentle bumping as the baby birds fell into one another. In a moment, the chirping and the scratching and the stranger were gone.

The diner was silent. The hot, dusty street was silent. Finally, somewhere down the sidewalk, a screen door opened and the loud banging of wood on wood reached our ears in the stillness of the humid room. The lunch rush had gone and the morning slowly rolled into the afternoon.

Harvard and Grant didn't talk at all now and Patsy looked nervous, as if she missed their complaining. She paced back and forth and dusted the cash register. She washed dishes that hadn't been dirtied. She searched the room for something out of place while I watched her, sipping my glass of water. I wanted to hold a baby chick again.

"The mouse is back," Jonny said suddenly. Bored, he pounded his electrical fan with a thump of his wrist. It whirred to life, and he grinned. His apron strings moved in the sudden breeze.

I turned to see Alpa standing at the window. I'd forgotten about her. Her long black hair hung loose and low, shadowing her rounded face. She shaded her eyes to see through the window. The sun had moved so that the diner's awning did nothing at all to shade the girl from the heat. Her dress fell limply around her form, a dress too warm for a hot summer day in 1969.

Alpa stared at me and waited. Her bike lay forgotten behind her on the sidewalk and the neighborhood dogs had returned. They chased their tails and bit at Alpa's shoes until she kicked one of them in the neck.

I should go.

"Patsy," Harvard grunted, suddenly. "Get that girl out of the sun."

Everyone sat surprised. No one from the Reservation had ever been in the diner before. Alpa had never been in the diner before. Harvard had never invited anyone anywhere at all.

Patsy finally waved a hand at Jonny. Jonny went out into the street to get the girl. He took Alpa's arm with hesitation and led her into the diner. Alpa, too surprised to protest, took her place by me. She sat straight, high on the warm, sticky stool. She seemed unsure and her eyes were wide as she stared uncertainly at Patsy's face. Patsy formed an O with her lips, her dry lipstick making a rough pink circle around her mouth.

And that was it. Harvard cleared his throat. He reached for one of Patsy's freshly baked pies and cut Alpa a healthy slice. He served it to her, ignoring his brother's stares and glaring at the patriot with the fan.

Alpa looked at Harvard curiously. She looked at me and then she smiled. She was pretty, sitting on her stool and eating apple pie.

"It's a warm one," Harvard said.

"You bet."

The Stacking Of Books In Four Movements

By E.K. Entrada

I fell in love with Chopin because of Piano Sonata No. 3. The name doesn't sound romantic, I'll admit, but if you've ever heard it, you would understand. Four movements: Allegro maestroso, Scherzo, Largo, Finale. It develops into a rising harmonic progression from a heavy beginning, then becomes melodic and bursts into an unsettling largo with subtle undertones. I learned the piece early, but didn't master it until my early 40s and even then I never really mastered it. It's been said to be one of the most difficult piano pieces to play; the only time I perform it in front of others is for the April brunch that I host for my middle-school students. The keys of my piano have been so beaten by my attempts at the sonata that the notes have settled into them.

It's no wonder that the sculptor Auguste Clesinger bronzed Chopin's hands after the composer died in 1849.

I wonder what my hands would look like if they were bronzed.

When I was ten years old, my piano teacher, Miss Gladys, turned my hands over and over in hers, looked at my mother, and proclaimed that I had the hands of a gifted pianist.

"Not all hands are made for the piano," Miss Gladys said to my mother, who proudly hovered over us and wondered why she had never noticed this before "See how slender her fingers are? See how long? That is perfect for playing the piano. I have students with short, stubby fingers and they have a difficult time because they can't arch them properly. To play the piano well, you have to know how to stroke the keys."

After piano recitals, Miss Gladys introduced me to adults in the gallery foyer and showed them my hands.

"Like a gifted pianist," she said.

That was forty-five years ago. Miss Gladys is long gone now. When I look at my hands today, I wonder what she would think of them. I wonder if they would make her cry. I wonder other things, too. Like how my hands would look if they were bronzed. Or how it would feel if they no longer existed at all.

***

That day – the day my hands started to disappear – began with pain. I'd had a dull ache in my fingers for months, but would never describe it as pain until that morning.

The pain and the sunlight descended on me at the same time as soon as I opened my eyes. I stretched my fingers – tried to, at least – to relieve some of the tension in my joints, but that made it worse. Shots of fire darted through my hands and I wailed.

Maybe I've been playing too much, I thought. I should take it easy.

The pain drifted away by mid-morning and instead of calling the doctor, I replaced the receiver without dialing and waited for my four o'clock student, Sabrina Melos, to arrive. Sabrina was twelve years old and struggling through her own version of Chopin's Piano Sonata No. 3 – "Portrait of a White Butterfly," by Wallace De Pue.

After three of her typical errors, she stopped playing and sighed.

"I should try something else," she said.

"Absolutely not," I said. "Keep going."

She played for a while longer, then stopped midway and rested her hands on her lap.

"Do you think I'm any good?" she asked.

"Absolutely."

"Could you play this song when you were a kid?"

"This composition didn't exist when I was a kid."

She giggled. "Sorry."

I grinned and nodded toward the piano. "Try again."

Sabrina rested her fingers on the keys. Took them off again. "What's wrong with your hands? You keep rubbing them."

I hadn't noticed, but when I looked down, she was right.

"They've been a little sore," I said.

"You should ask my dad about it." Her father was a doctor. "I bet he can tell you what's wrong."

"He's a gynecologist. I don't think it works that way." I tapped on the music book. "Back to your exercises."

When Sabrina's father picked her up thirty minutes later, she nudged his belly and pointed to my hands.

"Something's wrong with her hands," she said. "And she won't go to the doctor."

I chuckled and waved it off with burning fingers. "I told you not to bother your father about it, Sabrina. It's nothing. Probably just carpal tunnel syndrome."

Sabrina's father took long strides toward me and gently took my hands in his. He turned my hands over, just as Miss Gladys had done four decades earlier. I grimaced.

"Do they hurt in the morning?" he asked.

I nodded.

He brushed his fingertips across my knuckles. I grimaced again.

"I can recommend you to Dr. Hughes," he said. "You should see him."

He did, and I did.

***

When I close my eyes at the end of the day, after taking my Methotrexate, Planquenil and Azulfidine, I remember my visit to Dr. Hughes. The X-ray screen glows over his shoulder, and he tells me that I have rheumatoid arthritis, and I ask if I will still be able to play the piano, because this was before my fingers curled and stacked. Before my knuckles swelled.

He answers without answering.

The condition accelerated quickly. Maybe because I had acknowledged it; I'm not sure. The pain soon became unbearable and the medication made me dizzy and nauseous. When I told Dr. Hughes about it, he gave me more medicine.

"You should develop a pain management plan," he said. "When the medication doesn't work, try to relax and distract yourself from the pain. Avoid anxiety."

It's funny how the mind works. When he said "relax" and "avoid anxiety," I immediately made a mental note to spend more time at the piano, because that was how I relaxed. Then I remembered.

That afternoon, I called the parents of my students and told them I was retiring.

"Time to relax," I told Olivia Martin's mother. "I think I may travel. Spend some time seeing the world. I've been teaching piano for so long now, it's time for a change."

Like all the other parents, Mrs. Martin agreed that I needed a break. She congratulated me.

"I'm jealous," she said, and sighed. "I have years and years before I can retire."

"Don't worry," I said. "You'll get there."

Sabrina was the last person I called. I talked to her parents first, then to her.

"Who will teach me 'Butterfly'?" she asked. "I'll never learn it now."

"You will," I said.

"My parents said you're gonna travel. Where are you going?"

"I don't know yet."

"Do your hands still hurt?"

"A little."

When I finished calling the parents, I decided to clean the house – a good distraction, I told myself. I wiped down all the countertops and swept the kitchen. With the broom in my hand, I stood before my overstuffed bookcase and looked at all the stray books I'd stacked on the floor in front of it. I'd always planned to get a smaller bookcase for them, but I never did. Now I didn't need one.

I leaned the broom against the bookcase, gathered armloads of books, and stacked them on the piano bench. When I ran out of room on the bench, I stacked some underneath, near the foot pedals. When I ran out of room there, I stacked the rest on top of the piano itself.

***

Sometimes, when I close my eyes, I don't see the doctor. Instead, I hear Piano Sonata No. 3. Four movements: Allegro maestroso, Scherzo, Largo, finale. In life, it takes thirty minutes to perform, but I hear the sonata in seconds. Before Dr. Hughes and the X-rays, I heard the sonata the way I imagined Chopin would play it. Now I hear me. Even the errors.

At night, I sit on the couch, cover my hands with a blanket, and watch television. I tell myself that I'm going to travel. Go somewhere nice. Somewhere exotic, maybe. But I stay here, mostly.

Without my students, there isn't much happening at the house, which is why I was surprised to hear someone knocking on my door around seven o'clock one night, in the middle of a summer rerun. I walked to the door and peered through the crackled glass. It had been months since I had seen Sabrina, but I could tell it was her by the outline of her ribbon, the way she stood, and the silhouette of her father standing next to her.

When I opened the door, she immediately hugged me and asked how I was doing.

"Just fine," I said, smiling. "What brings you here?"

"I have a surprise for you," she said. "Hand-delivered."

I examined both of them. "I don't see any gifts. Unless it's that sedan in the driveway."

Sabrina giggled. "Not exactly."

I stepped aside and they walked in, as if it was four o'clock and time for a lesson.

"Have you gone anywhere exciting on your retirement?" Sabrina asked. Her father followed on her heels.

"Not quite, but there are things in the works."

"How are your hands?" her father asked.

I put them behind my back and shrugged. "Not great, but sometimes it's not too bad."

He nodded silently.

"So," I said, to Sabrina. "Where's this big surprise?"

"You have to follow me to the piano room first," she said, and before I could stop her, she sprinted to the room and flicked the light switch. The lights had been off for so long that my eyes had to adjust. As soon as they came on, Sabrina gasped.

The three of us stood there for a long time, staring at the buried piano and its massive stacks of hardcovers and paperbacks, without saying a word. Finally Sabrina walked to the piano bench, gathered an armful of books, and stacked them in the corner. She went back, took another armful, put them in the corner. Her father joined in. They passed each other, back and forth, carrying and stacking. I watched from the doorway as my piano was unearthed. When the deed was done, her father joined me in the doorway and Sabrina stood in front of the piano bench and bowed.

"Thank you for coming, ladies and gentlemen," she said. "I would like to present 'A Portrait of a White Butterfly,' by Wallace de Pue."

She bowed again, sat on the bench, and played.

Sweet Revenge

By Bill Charles

Betty didn't need an alarm clock. For years she detested the rude intrusion of the electric devices. One sat atop the night stand next to the bed in the master bedroom but it was used only on those occasions when Rodney had to catch an early flight. Otherwise, it served no other purpose than as a digital time piece. Betty's alarm clock was internal. Her body knew when she had rested sufficiently and she simply woke up gradually, naturally and usually between 7:30 and 8:00 each morning. Since she and Rodney were self-employed consultants and the sole proprietors of "Fosters, Inc.," they were in the enviable position to set their own schedules rather than adhere to the whims and demands of an employer. They enjoyed the freedom and amenities of owning their own business and they prospered as well.

Monday morning was like most mornings. The sun's early morning rays crept quietly into bedroom and settled gently upon Betty's face. She stirred, stretching first her arms and then her legs. She relaxed momentarily and then repeated the ritual again. It felt good to first tighten and then relax her muscles in such fashion. She shrugged her head from side to side to loosen the tendons in her upper back and those between her shoulder blades. Finally, she opened her eyes slightly. The bright sunlight penetrated the narrow slits behind which her pupils shied away from the glare. She shut her eyelids tightly, waiting several seconds before opening them again, this time wider than before. The blur of the morning finally began to melt away. Betty glanced at the clock: 7:38. Perfect!

She sat up in bed listening for the familiar sound of her husband typing on the personal computer. There was no sound.

Perhaps he's on the deck, she thought, or in the bathroom. He may also be out jogging as he does most days, although he's usually finished his daily exercise by 7:00.

She reached for the robe that lay at the foot of the bed. It was her favorite and had been a gift from her one true friend, Amy. The blanket in which she had been comfortably wrapped fell to her waist. Her shoulders, exposed by the spaghetti straps of her delicate night gown, recoiled in the coolness of the morning. She quickly donned the robe, buttoning each button. It took only seconds for her shoulders to feel the difference. As she rose from bed, the thought crossed her mind that a warm embrace from Rodney would provide even more warmth than the robe.

"Rodney," she called. There was no answer. "He must still be jogging," she murmured audibly.

After brushing her teeth, Betty started downstairs. Halfway down the stairs, she paused. Something was missing. Continuing her descent, she realized that the aroma of freshly brewed coffee was absent. Rodney always made coffee as soon as he awoke each day. She had just restocked the pantry on Saturday so she knew their supply had not run out.

She entered the kitchen. The coffee pot was off and still held the remains from the previous evening. That was odd. He hadn't even cleaned the pot much less brewed some coffee.

The breakfast table caught her eye. There was no newspaper as there always is when she wakes up. She peaked through the large kitchen window overlooking the raised, wooden deck. Nothing. Not a sign of Rodney.

"Rodney!" Still no answer.

She began to feel a bit unnerved. This wasn't like her husband at all. He was always considerate. If he had to leave for an early morning appointment with a client, he'd let her know the night before or, if it slipped his mind the previous evening, he would leave her a note telling her where he was going and what time he expected to return. There was no note this morning.

Betty started back up the stairs. Perhaps he's fallen asleep in the converted bedroom that served as their office.

She opened the door. Rodney was not on the couch, nor was he at the desk. She stood in the doorway, peering in, puzzled by her husband's absence. She stared at nothing in particular for several moments, her mind trying to discern what was happening.

"Where is he," she asked aloud. She often spoke aloud and this habit, on many occasions, resulted in others attempting to respond to her subconscious questions or statements made public. It was a nuisance not only to her but to those in earshot of her remarks.

Suddenly it hit her. The computer, printer and file cabinet were missing. So were the many clientele binders they had compiled over the fifteen years they had been in business. The office looked naked. Why hadn't she noticed that when she first opened the door? It was all so obvious now.

A small white envelope on top of the desk caught her eye. A wave of nausea enveloped her as she walked toward the desk. She reached for it, her hands trembling as she picked up the envelope which was addressed simply, "Betty."

Even after eight months, Betty hurt. What had gone wrong in their marriage? Why had Rodney deserted her after twenty years of marriage. Who was the other woman in his life? She struggled often with questions like these. What could she have done to prevent the breakup of her marriage? Rodney was typically out of town on business several times each month. Should she have accompanied him, if only occasionally? She painstakingly searched her memory for signs, for anything that would have provided a clue that their marriage was at risk, but each time, she came up empty handed. The suddenness of it all haunted her. Even now, she could recall the horror of reading the piercing words of the note he left behind.

> *Dear Betty,*
>
> *I don't know how to say this in an easy fashion so I'll be as concise as possible. I have fallen out of love with you. I'm in love with another. You've been great to me for twenty years and I appreciate the love you've shared and all you've done for me. But, I can't continue in our marriage. Please understand that the fault lies not with you but with my own weaknesses.*
>
> *Rodney*

In love with another! All you've done for me! His words knifed through her.

"The bastard," she yelled. "He didn't even have the courage to tell me to my face!"

She recalled their last Sunday evening together. They ate dinner and then enjoyed a quiet evening. After two glasses of red zinfandel, she had begun to feel amorous and pursued him flirtatiously, seducing him until he succumbed to her advances and they made love on the floor of the den in front of the fire place. The thought of that passionate moment now turned her stomach. What a fool she'd been! How could Rodney go through with the greatest act of intimacy knowing all along that in a matter of hours he would pack his belongings and sneak away to wherever his "another" might be. She felt betrayed by the man she had loved for so many years, by the man who knew every intimate detail of her life and who would not have achieved financial success without her support and assistance.

How in the hell did he manage to pack and leave without awakening her that night, she wondered. She wasn't drunk by any means. She had gone to bed around 10:00 PM, tired yet feeling good about herself. She fell asleep easily and apparently soundly.

Rodney had managed to slip into their bedroom, pack most of his clothes, disconnect the computer and accessories and load everything, including the two drawer file cabinet into his Jeep Cherokee. How did he do it, she thought.

The thought crossed her mind that perhaps the other woman helped him. She was repulsed by the idea that her husband's lover may have been tip-toeing stealthily in her bedroom and in their office while she slept soundly. Rodney probably told his lover that he had to make love to her only hours before. Her stomach turned.

In the ensuing months since Rodney left, Betty had not heard from him. Her only contact with Rodney was through her attorney and his. She had come to the conclusion that she would never hear from Rodney. The first month following his sudden departure was difficult. She became severely depressed and withdrawn. There were periods when she wouldn't leave her bedroom for days at a time except to go to the bathroom to relieve herself or to the kitchen for nourishment. One week, she didn't cook or prepare her own food. Instead, she ordered delivery service from one of several local establishments. Friends would call but she wasn't in the mood to talk. She didn't even find comfort in the long, warm baths that used to help her unwind and relax. But, Betty was a pragmatist at heart. Finally, after four weeks, she forced herself to return to some semblance of her previous schedule. It struck her one day that she had not cleaned the house in weeks. Even the delivery containers from the local pizzeria, Steak Out and a Chinese Food restaurant were still stacked on every surface of the kitchen. Enough was enough she decided. Rodney wasn't coming back so she had better get her life in gear again.

After tackling the kitchen, she started on the rest of the house. First, she vacuumed and dusted the den, cleaned the bathrooms and finally, she decided to clean the bedroom, the place where she and Rodney had spent so many intimate evenings. She surveyed the room and decided to give it a complete cleaning and makeover. Not only would she vacuum, dust and clean the molding but, she would replace the window curtains and the bedspread as well. She wanted to exorcize anything that might remind her of her husband.

Betty was on the petite side but she was strong, thanks to the Spartan exercise regimen she had maintained for fifteen years. Not only did she run and bike, but she worked out with weights and really enjoyed that form of exercise. So, when she had to move the bulky chest of drawers, she thought nothing of doing so herself. Yes, it was heavy, but she knew how to leverage her weight and strength to move the piece of furniture so that she could clean behind it.

Once she moved it a sufficient distance to allow her to reach easily behind it, she noticed something on the floor. She bent down and immediately recognized that it was a key to the safety deposit box that she and Rodney had rented for years at the main branch of 1st Tennessee Bank. They used the lock box to store stocks they owned in various companies. They had decided to liquidate the stocks months ago and Rodney told her that once they did so, they wouldn't have need of the lock box. He told her he would cancel the rental. But, they couldn't locate Betty's key. Apparently, it was lost. Now that she had it in hand, she decided to return it to the bank the next time she had need to visit it.

It was Monday morning and Betty had several errands to run. She needed to stock the pantry, buy some vegetable and meat products and several toiletries. She planned to stop at Marge's Salon. She needed a cut and also wanted to have her graying hair high-lighted. She remembered the key to the safety deposit box. She would pass the bank on her way to Marge's so, she would stop and drop the key off.

Since it was the first work day of the week, the bank was rather crowded with business people depositing their takes from the weekend. Betty was glad she didn't have to stand in the tellers' lines. Instead, there was a separate desk for, among other things, customers to access their safety deposit boxes. As Betty approached the desk, she had a sudden thought. Why not see if the box was still registered in her and Rodney's name.

"Can I help you," the clerk asked.

Betty told her she wanted to get into a lock box and handed her the key. The clerk searched the 3 X 5 metal file at the desk and retrieved the signature card.

"Are you Mrs. Foster?"

"Yes, I am." There may be another Mrs. Foster soon, she thought, but Foster was still her married name for now.

The clerk handed Betty the card and asked her to sign and date it.

As Betty signed the card, she noticed that Rodney had signed the card every month since he was to have cancelled the box. She was puzzled but she also became very curious. The clerk accompanied her into the vault and using the master key and the key Betty provided, she unlocked the box.

"Take your time, Mrs. Foster." She left the vault.

Betty placed the box on the small metal table that was toward the back end of the vault. She found it odd, but her pulse rate had increased noticeably. She opened the box. At first, the cash that stared back at her did not register. She simply stared at it for several seconds. Finally, it hit her. "Damn!" The word escaped her lips but was not loud enough to be heard outside the vault. What in the hell is this, she wondered. She began removing the money from the box. It was mostly 100 dollar bills but there were also a few 1000 dollar bills.

She didn't know what to do. Surely, Rodney had put the cash in the box but why and where did it come from? Their clients paid by check, the accepted means for conducting business. She wondered if Rodney had been up to something illegal. Her body shook as she tried to decide what to do. Should she leave the cash in the box and pretend she never saw it? Should she contact local law enforcement and turn it over to them? She was in a quandary. Finally, it occurred to her that she and Rodney were still legally married and that the box was still registered in both their names. She rationalized that, at worst, she might be considered as part owner of the cash. She immediately began stuffing her large purse with cash. She also had a plastic bag in her purse from an errand she had run earlier that morning. She stuffed more cash into the bag. After emptying the box, Betty returned the box to its place in the vault. She tried not to be conspicuous as she left with the plastic bag in her arms.

"Thank you," she quipped to the clerk and left the bank quickly.

Her heart was pounding by now. To hell with the hair cut, she thought. And, she could survive another day with the food and supplies she had on hand. She wanted to get home fast. She made an effort to drive safely. She had no intentions of being pulled over for a traffic offense.

Betty sat at the table and for several minutes she simply stared at the cash. "Rodney," she asked, "what in the hell have you been up to?"

She decided to count the money, placing the $100 bills in stacks of $1000. After completing this task, she began to count the stacks. She counted two hundred stacks. There were also eight $1000 bills. In all, she counted $208,000. She recounted to ensure she had not miscounted. The second count was the same as the first. Betty then stuffed the money into a large, black trash bag.

It was a long night. Betty didn't sleep well. Her mind just wouldn't quiet down. She thought of the large sum of money and wondered how Rodney had accumulated it. She became convinced that Rodney had done something illegal. After all, she reasoned, why wouldn't he have deposited the cash in an account? Was he into drugs or money laundering? She didn't know. What she did know was that legally, at least half the money belonged to her since they were not yet divorced.

She tossed and turned most of the night, falling asleep for brief periods. She took a Tylenol PM to calm her mind but her mind was overwhelmed with a barrage of thoughts, visions and fears. Ever since Rodney had left unannounced, she had become a victim of numerous fears, most of which were unfounded. Every unexpected sound in the house was magnified whether caused by the refrigerator ice machine or the sound of pine cones falling from the seven southern pine trees in the backyard. Her fears drove her to buy a homeless German shepherd from the local SPCA. When she first saw the dog she thought its size and bark alone would make it a good watchdog. She was told that it went by the name of Rambette, a feminine play on the name Rambo. The dog was friendly to her so she bought it for the cost of inoculations.

During one of her brief sleep episodes, she dreamt she was in the back yard and had started a fire in the 55 gallon drum Rodney would use to burn trash and fallen pine cones. In the dream, she threw something, perhaps trash, into the drum. As she burned whatever it was she was burning, a smile graced her lips. When Betty awoke, she recalled the dream vividly and wondered what, if anything, the dream might mean.

She was drinking her second cup of coffee when the dream's meaning became clear to her. She hurriedly gulped the last of the coffee. She had work to do.

Rodney showed his driver's license to the clerk at the bank. She compared it to what was on file and determined that Rodney was who he said he was. She retrieved the signature index card and asked him to sign. As Rodney began to sign the card, he noticed Betty's signature dated the day before. His hand began to quiver.

"Is this a mistake," he asked, showing the card to the clerk and pointing at Betty's signature.

"No sir. In fact, Mrs. Foster was in here yesterday."

Without another word, Rodney signed the card and handed his key to the clerk. The clerk escorted him into the vault and retrieved the safety deposit box.

"Take as much time as you need, Mr. Foster."

Rodney nodded without looking at her. As soon as she left the room, he opened the box. His fears became a reality as he stared into a near empty box. Only his passport and birth certificate remained. His heart rate jumped significantly and he breathed heavily. He returned the box to its slot and exited quickly.

"That was quick, Mr. Foster," the clerk said to him. Rodney didn't acknowledge her as he left in a hurry.

Rodney could hardly contain himself as he drove to the house he had shared with Betty for so many years. His mind was in a quandary. Why did she go into the box? What had she done with the money? How would his dealer respond if the money was missing? Rodney bought cocaine from a high school acquaintance. The acquaintance was convinced that NARCS were on his tail and that the IRS was snooping around his financial records. He only wanted to store the cash safely for six to nine months before moving it to another account or safe place. Fortunate for him that Rodney offered the use of the safety box, one which he was to cancel months earlier. Now that the money was missing, Rodney feared that his former high school buddy might not look so kindly upon it.

Rodney drove above the speed limit. A traffic ticket was the least and last thing on his mind. As he neared the house, he saw that Betty's car was parked in the driveway rather than the garage.

At least he knew she was probably home. He parked his car haphazardly, partially in the driveway and partially in the grass. He was much too hurried to care about it.

He rang the doorbell several times. No one answered. He knocked and still no one came to the door. He knocked harder and suddenly a dog barked. It sounded as if the barking had come from the back yard. He walked around the house and Rambette rushed the fence, barking and growling at the stranger. He then noticed Betty as she threw a lit match into the rusty 55 gallon drum. The flame quickly rose due to the paper, wood and gasoline she had poured into the drum.

"Betty," he called out. She looked up from her chore. If she was surprised to see Rodney, she didn't show it. In fact, she smiled to acknowledge him.

"Hi Rodney. You've been gone so long, what on earth brings you here today?"

Rodney tried to hide the anger in his voice and face.

"I think you know why I'm here. You took something yesterday that didn't belong to you."

"And what was that," she replied coyly.

"You know damned well what you took. I don't think you want to involve yourself in something like this."

Rambette detected anger in Rodney's voice. She began to bark and growl more loudly.

"And when in the hell did you get a dog?"

Betty continued to throw paper and cones into the drum. "First, why I bought a dog is none of your damned business. But, if you would like to personally meet Rambette, please jump the fence. I assure you her bite is worse than her bark."

Rodney looked down at the apoplectic dog. He had no desire to meet her anymore than he had done already.

"Second, the safety deposit box is still listed as a joint account. So, the box and the contents are just as much mine as yours. And, since you left and took our computer and files and who knows what else, I thought I might do likewise with what was in the safety deposit box."

Rodney's anger showed. "You can't do that to me. That was not my money. I was holding it for someone. He would be awfully angry if you stole it. You wouldn't want that."

The fire was now raging. Betty lifted a black garbage bag that was beside her. Slowly she unloosened the red straps on the black bag. Opening the bag, she began to dump the cash into the flames. Rodney was beside himself. He started to jump the fence but Rambette began leaping at him, snarling and barking, anxious to sink her teeth into the intruder.

Betty stared at him. Her sardonic smile grew wider. She continued to empty the cash into the small inferno.

"Well, Rodney, I think you will have a difficult time explaining to someone where the money is." The bag was empty now and she threw it into the flames. "Now, how are you going to prove I took the money?"

Rodney watched in horror as the flame grew higher. His face turned white and a wave of nausea engulfed him. Betty had him by the balls and he knew it. He couldn't complain to the bank. After all, the deposit box was in her name also. Besides, he could never convince bank officials that he had hidden over two hundred thousand dollars in the box. He couldn't complain to the police. How could he account for a large sum of money sitting idly in a safety deposit box? Worse still, how could he hope to explain to his dealer that his estranged wife had taken the cash? Rodney had assured the dealer that only he, Rodney, had access to the box.

Betty had exacted her revenge on her estranged husband and revenge was sweet.

Oh, Amanda, How I Will Reclaim Thee

By Ryan Sayles

My only true love was stolen from me long ago. I'm talking decades. Some other dude swooped in when I was too young, too foolish, too mixed up to do anything about it and snatched her from me.

Her name is Amanda, and to this day, I long for her. I pine for her. I hold a candle for her. Crave would be a right word. Lust after would be a right phrase. Also: be desirous of, bay after, kill for, give my right arm for, want with all my heart, and yearn after.

And: will have one day.

She called me not too long ago-we keep in touch thank God-telling me about her pending divorce. She was devastated, her husband walking in and just telling her one day that he was leaving with another woman. A younger woman. A woman who hadn't spit out three kids and been worn down by years of no sleep, cold meals and perpetual messes. What a fool. What an ass. He used her up and then, when they should have been traveling together, blowing money, seeing the sights and finally enjoying life, he rejects her. His loss. One man's trash is another man's treasure.

No younger woman would replace Amanda with me. None ever have. I have never married on account of being hung up on her. Devotion drives me. It is my discipline. I don't think she knows this-I have never told her for fear of hurting her-and if she does, she has never admitted it. I am saving myself for her. My virginity, my one true gift, my chastity, it will be hers if she chooses to accept it. And I think she will.

I remember the first time I saw her. She was in a housedress, handkerchief in her hair and a long, brilliant blonde ponytail dangling from the back. She wasn't wearing make-up; she didn't need any. Her eyes an azure blue, flecks of jewels cast inside her iris to make them gleam and hypnotize. She was so young then.

Her lips have always been full, even at her age now. Her smile still bright. I could just kill that sonofabitch for what he did to me. I could kill him for what he has done to her. I could kill him and don't you think for a second that I haven't spent entire nights... oh, I guess the police would call it "scheming" or "plotting." "Pre-meditating." I call it "just desserts." I call it "re-claiming what was mine from the get-go."

His name is Paul. I should throw that out there. Paul the Divorcer. Paul the Adulterer. Paul the Achilles Heel. My Achilles Heel. Paul and Amanda. My dream couple, only with my head placed over his. That's the way I have it in all the pictures they've given me of themselves over the years. The years I've been lying in wait. Passing time. "Scheming."

Sometimes they'll come over and I have to take all their pictures down because once, I went to one of those photo booths in the mall that eject a whole long string of photos and I took pictures like six separate times to make sure I had enough, and I put those head-shots of mine over all of Paul's. I was smiling, Amanda was smiling, Paul was gone and everything was the way it should be. Bliss, my friends. Bliss.

They had three kids. I think I've already mentioned this. Joey, Caroline and Steven.

Joey is my favorite. Bright kid, going places. Grown up now. He never went to college and never needed to. Things come his way it seems like. He makes ends meet and is a really good-looking guy. Chicks stare at him as he walks down the street. Just can't keep their eyes off of him. People get out of his way. Never married, never needed to, I guess. But he's athletic, charming, going places.

Amanda confessed to me one day that while she "has no favorites" among her children, Joey has a special place with her. Me being the oldest myself, that tells me a lot about how she feels about him. Good kid.

Caroline is drab and dull. She sucks the life out of parties and get-togethers. She skulks and lurks about, as if she were a harmless, inept zombie who had nothing better to do than stand over your shoulder and breathe heavily. Poor sense of humor. Poor posture. Poor complexion and hygiene. She acts beaten down although she's never really had a relationship, let alone an abusive one.

I did try and get with her for a little while when I figured her mom was not into me. It was just a phase. My darkest place in life. Since I was approaching Caroline like that, it is obvious I didn't care about myself.

Anyways, the reasons are unimportant. I came on to her. She acted all grossed out and wouldn't talk to me for a long, long time. I tried explaining it away, saying that I was drunk and confused and thought she was somebody else and it would ruin everything if she told anybody, especially her mother. I guess she's never said anything.

I thought about threatening her if she did, something really violent and disturbing, but like I said, it seems like she's kept her mouth shut.

Did I mention I'm on my way over to Amanda's house right now? I offered to come over and 'console' her. She said she'd really like that and I almost hung up on her I darted off the phone and out my front door so fast. I'll show her what 'console' means. I am the luckiest man alive.

Steven is likeable enough. He and I get along, but our relationship has never been that close. Age gap, I guess. He's a spitting image of his father: medium height, barrel-chested, spindly black hairs coming out of his shirt collar, good with pipe-fitting and plumbing. Married, divorced. Married again. One kid. A little brat who thinks that, because she has two homes, two mommies and two daddies (Steven's first wife remarried also) the whole world should just keep on throwing her everything it's got. Bitch. And only five years old, too. Ruined already. Sad if you think about it.

But my Amanda just dotes over her only grandchild. She is beyond her years of childbearing, but I figure we just found ourselves late in life and we can enjoy other things. I'll wait until the ink is dry on the divorce papers before I propose. That's honorable. She is worth waiting for. She has been all these years. All these long, dark, irretrievable years. Don't get me wrong; I'll sleep with her tonight if she's into it, but becoming engaged to her? Only a conniving trollop accepts a proposition from another man while she still belongs to another.

Gross. My Amanda is not such a woman.

I figure the first thing we will do when we tie the knot is burn down the house she and Paul lived in. Obvious enough, it seems. It represents too much to me to leave it standing. For a long time I figured the same fate would befall the church that married them also, but now, thinking with a much clearer head and better perspective, I think if that same church married she and I it would even out. Makes sense.

Of course I'd make sure every last trace of Paul was inside the inferno as it goes up. We can make our own home, our own memories at my house or even buy a third, new-to-the-both-of-us place. But I will not fill wherever that winds up being with evidence of him. Why start off on a leg that bad?

If she wants to adopt I'll let her. I could use a boy to raise. I think I would make a good man out of somebody, so I'm OK with that idea. Plus, if it makes her happy I want it. And another plus: she's got some big bones in her savings account so the price of buying a child wouldn't hit my wallet too hard. I don't see a downside. Childrearing with your one true love is a gift. She deserves that. And I get to mold a boy in my own image.

I'm here! Pulling my car into her driveway just brings back so many memories. A tide of them. Pick-up basketball games, Fourth of July, barbeques. Summers and winters speed through my mind like time-lapse photography. Leaves bud and spread, turn green, then orange, red and brown, fall off as its branch gets coated in snow. The snow twinkles in sunlight and thins out, disappears. Another bud pops up.

In my front seat I have a plastic sack. I grab it and tie a knot in the top, sealing it off from prying eyes. If one were to look in there, see the roll of duct tape, the folded sheet of plastic, the condom, the knife, the bottle of pills, the other, more unmentionable things, one might get the wrong idea.

I step out and have to fight down the butterflies in my stomach. Excitement buzzes every nerve and I just want to sing. To sing! This moment, I was born for. This moment, I was destined for, even prior to being placed in the womb. This is my life's culmination right here, right now.

I walk up her steps and ring the doorbell. So familiar. The chime is as known to me as my own voice, dinging four notes that welcome and announce. I breathe in deeply and smash a piece of gum into my mouth. In the reflection in the glass, I straighten my shirt and fiddle with my hair before I hear the knob turn.

The door opens. She stands there, a radiant glow about her. An angel. Her eyes puffy from crying but the relief-no, the joy! The absolute joy!-in them at seeing me shines through. I am the luckiest man alive.

I have waited a lifetime for this. I would have waited a hundred. I should have killed Paul all those years ago. I've had nothing but chances. Oh well. Everything comes to he who waits.

"Hi, Joey." She says to me and kisses my cheek. Her soft, cool hand caresses my face and she exudes her love for me.

"Hi Amanda. I was worried about you."

"Mom, sweetheart." She says in that musical voice of hers like she has said for my whole life. "I'm your mother, dear, call me that."

I say sure and I follow her inside.

"What's in your bag?" she asks as the front door closes us off from the outside world.

You Hipster Douchebags Have Gone Too Far

By Caroline Burman

Drneeeaaawww…drenooaaaawww….

The thick strings on the bass guitar stretched and released and buzzed as I tuned them. I sat on the floor of my nearly empty and fully decrepit flat; focusing on the strings. Tonight is just like any other night, I sighed. Alone. I hadn't been with a woman since Uni, 5 years ago. I've tried. Brought them up to my room to drink, play old records, see what would happen, yet nothing ever did. They left every time. I forced down a cheap beer and closed my eyes. Let my fingers detach themselves, float away into another dimension to bring back the pulsating language that can only be found deep within those well-worn King Crimson albums. I played along to the skips. I picked that up as a kid, a technique that was put to use several years ago, playing punk-jazz to puking students. Isolation, that's the thing for me now. Waiting tables, gaining money that's barely spent. Rent is cheap, the restaurant is popular, and eating is overrated anyway. I don't socialize much at work. I do what I need to do. People come to eat. I refuse to tumble out of the kitchen balancing a firecracker on my dick just to get a good tip, and I feel that I am respected for it.

I own a telephone, but no activity has been coming from it since my birthday, several months ago, and even then the only call was my mother. A friend came over unannounced and we got drunk and ended up eating raw hot dogs.

I saw the dust explode into the air before I heard the shrill shrieking of the phone that made me cringe. What the f*ck is that? I thought.

Cautiously, I brought the phone to my ear

"…Ahoy?"

"Arthur?" A man. Curses!

"Yeeeessssss…?"

"It's me! Ken!"

We had eaten raw hot dogs in the pale moonlight. I remember. Ken had left for the United States ridiculously abruptly around 4 months ago.

"Hey. How are you?"

"I'm getting married!" He shouted, clearly ecstatic in a way I had never seen him. He was always so melancholy. He wore neckties for no apparent reason. I was unsure of how to react. Well, not especially. Had we been face-to-face, I would most likely have shouted congratulations, and given him an awkward man-hug. I loathe telephones.

"Great!"

I felt underwhelmed.

"It's the American women, Arthur. They love us. We're like peacocks. You're still single? You've got to come here. Stay with me for a while."

"Are you suggesting that if I come to the States…I'm going to have some sort of godlike status among women?"

"Absolutely."

I hated sounding desperate.

I hated being desperate.

I hated being Morrissey.

"Up and let's go." I declared.

                                    ***

Plans are for neo-Nazi fascists. I packed up, planning to be gone for a month, barely nabbed a ticket to Newark, New Jersey, and alerted my boss the evening before.

Ken agreed to pick me up with his future wife. I was prepared for sitting in a corner while the man I once knew mastered no speech outside of "No, you're Schmoopy!"

Fuck fuck fuck.

I slept on the plane.

I woke up to find that I had somehow managed to get off the plane and was now riding in a car with my friend who wore the very first Smiths LP out completely, and a bended-out coat hanger with a head. She chattered a bit, with the rhythm of a woodpecker, and I did not listen. Marrying people for sex seems like amputating a foot because of a wart. I wanted so badly to say so.

But I remembered. I haven't had sex in 4 years. Desperate times.

Ken helped me slug my shit up the steep stairs, and dropped it on the floor beside the couch. I didn't mind sleeping there. Kate didn't live with him; praise Jesus, Allah, Vishnu, Cthulu. However, it was her idea to drag me out to dinner. Working in a restaurant is nothing especially terrible, but sitting in one, wading through that insipid chatter, how awful it is. I quickly showered and redressed in a clean t-shirt/jeans combination. I pulled my hair back with a stale rubber band.

Ken and I waited. Kate had to apply another layer of makeup. I assumed that this was to conceal the fact that she was, in reality, some sort of scaled, lizard carnivore creature. Awkwardness filled the room.

Ken cleared his throat, and then I cleared mine. Our throats went back and forth in a game of ping-pong. Kate reemerged from the bathroom, causing Ken and I to stand up straight in unison. They linked fingers, and I trailed behind, watching their pink, conjoined hand globe bob up and down all the way to a dumpy bar & grill.

It was empty. A girl seated us straight away, and my eyes strained in the annoyingly dim lights.

"So what do you do?" Kate bared her bleached teeth at me in an expression of friendliness, or perhaps hunger.

"I'm a waiter right now. Aspiring musician."

"Mm-hmm. What instrument do you play?" She rested her chin on her fists.

"Bass guitar."

She nodded.

A thin, dark-haired, heavily made-up girl sauntered to our table.

"Hi! My name's Kristi, I'll be your waitress tonight. Can I start you off with anything to drink?"

Alcohol for all. We decided to order our meals as well.

"Just a salad, thanks." Being a strict vegetarian as I was, this type of establishment offered little else in the way of slaughter-free meals.

"Uh-huh," she wrote the order down and added, "Hey, are you from England?"

Here it comes.

"Yeah, I am."

"Oh, wow, cool! When did you come here?"

"This morning", I said. "Just visiting for about a month or so."

"Sweet! Well, hey, I'll be right back with your orders."

Ken kicked my shin lightly under the table.

"I think you should go for it, Arthur."

Kate added, "That girl is totally into you!"

"I'm supposed to ask out some girl I know absolutely nothing about because she finds it interesting that I'm from another country?" I asked.

"YES!" Ken and Kate answered in unison, a moment that made me feel nauseated. Perhaps it was my unwillingness to bombard strangers with date offers that had left me alone. The Kristi creature returned, and because the restaurant was empty, she hung around, hovering around my seat like a mosquito.

"So what's your name?" she began the questionnaire.

"Arthur". I took a long drink.

"What do you do?"

"Actually, the same exact thing as you. I'm a waiter." I added self-consciously, in case she moonlighted in the sex industry.

"Oh wow!" I could hear her inner monologue shouting "we have so much in common!"

"So," I knew this line would work, "Are you a bad musician or a bad actor?"

She laughed. "No, I'm in college! I'm a business major."

I nodded. "I'm a musician." I tried to impress her.

"Oh cool! Do you play guitar?"

"I play a bass."

She looked puzzled.

"It's like a guitar," I explained, "except it has 4 strings instead of 6, and the pitches are lower." She seemed interested. "That's awesome," she smiled, revealing giant white teeth. I nodded again as she went back to get our food.

God, she was sexy.

Ken and Kate only watched me, looking on sweetly. I formulated what to say in my head.

"Sooooo…" I'd say, "What are you doing tomorrow?"

And it worked.

"Oh, nothing," she giggled, "why?"

"Do you want to go do something?" I asked politely.

"Oh sure! I'll show you all around town!" she grinned.

Ken grinned. "I told you!" he shouted as Kristi walked away. She had given me her telephone number, with the promise of being at Ken's apartment tomorrow at 4.

"You see?" Kate said. "That was easy!"

"I know." I was not expecting torture worthy of a Franz Kafka story. Ken only looked at me as if to say told you. I didn't want to end up like him. I just wanted a free lunch! I remembered the days when Ken and I would tell each other things like this. He would have nodded and said "TANSTAAFL!" No more.

He's an adult now, I thought mockingly. I thought of what tomorrow's date would bring. This girl was just like Kate. Different hair, but underneath it was the same vapid expression and lack of any personality. I will never be happy with such a woman. I poked around my salad, sinking deeper into a strange hybrid of hopelessness and excitement. Perhaps she was faking her insipidness? Perhaps within that shell of makeup was someone sarcastic and bitter and just like me, only with fantastic breasts! Despite the fact that this fantasy was incredibly unlikely, I decided to cling to it.

***

I woke up around 10:00 the next morning, and Ken had made coffee. I dislike coffee, but I drank some anyway. I had been up late the night before, pacing around and making sure that my lines were just perfect: clever enough to cause this girl to be enamored with me, but not so clever that she would become frightened.

"Good morning!" Ken sang. Jesus Christ. My best friend wouldn't sing! And if he did, he would only sing Bauhaus!

I nodded at him. I poured myself a bowl of cereal and sat down.

"Are you excited for today?" he asked.

"I guess so." I don't get excited about anything. Ken used to know that.

"How are you going to dress?" he asked.

"How am I supposed to dress?"

"Well, I don't know, Arthur. Maybe she'd take you someplace nice."

"Ken you don't get it. People in the food service industry are not wealthy people. We do not take people we barely know to 'someplace nice.' I consider discount movie theaters to be wonderful dates. Not that I've been on one in a while." I complained.

Ken didn't say anything, but I could see his thoughts radiating in his eyes like a scrolling marquee: YOU NEED TO BE FUCKED.

I knew it. I wondered if vacant women found homemade Can t-shirts sexy. I'd take the risk. I showered and took a surprising amount of time to construct a look that said "I don't care; love me." Ken and I watched television in near-silence. We filled the time.

4:00 came, and Kristi was standing at the door.

"Hey, you! Ready to go?" she grinned and her head seemed to twitch in a birdlike motion.

"Um...yeah." I waved goodbye to Ken, and she quickly linked her arm through mine. She smelled excellent. We meandered aimlessly, and she asked me about myself. I tried to paint myself as cool. She bought it. She knew nothing about everything, so a foreign fellow with a limited scope of knowledge was wildly impressive in her world.

"What about you?" I asked.

"Oh, not much happens to me," she assured me, "I became a business major because I didn't know what else to do. My job is boring. I watch TV a lot, because there isn't much else for me to do."

Her pathetic ways were insanely adorable.

"So hey," she said, "I'm tired of walking. We could go to my house and watch TV or something."

She moved fast. She gripped my hand and led me up the stairs to her flat. It was nearly as empty as my own. We sat awkwardly on the couch. She turned on the TV, but looked at me as she did so. She wanted me to kiss her, I guessed. I did, and it was awkward and stilted. She laughed. Oh ho ho, I could hear her thinking, I'll show you how to do it. We went back at it. I could feel her artificial hair gleaming under my fingers. Her hands moved up and down my back, then moved to my ribs. We were wretchedly bored. There was no music; there was no romance, only the suffocating boredom of two people and a television with nothing on.

As we were tearing off our clothes in an animalistic display of bored passion, she revealed that she liked to chat during these activities. I decided to go along, and we talked about current events, until we moved onto films.

"So," she said in a gasping breath after her mouth broke free from my shoulder. "Are all British movies as funny as Four Weddings and a Funeral?"

Oh no.

Oh no.

I felt everything slipping away. I stood up, naked and unashamed. Such a creature didn't even deserve me. She stared up at me.

"What?" she asked in a near-laugh.

Does this woman know anything? I wondered. I had no idea why this comment created such a response in me. My life became news-clippings on documentaries about serial killers.

"It just kind of happened."

I became angry, and she was dead. The cultural plebian. I choked her and threw her down the stairs leading to the door. I walked back up, put my clothes back on and left, hoping that the next day would yield less stupid romantic possibilities.

Being good with directions, I was able to make the walk back to Ken's apartment with ease. He let me in, and we sat down to some beers.

"How'd it go?" he asked.

"It was all right. But-get this. She liked to talk during sex! So we were starting up, and she started talking about movies, and how funny she thought Four Weddings and a Funeral was, and my tastes were grossly offended and I killed her."

"Ah," he said after a sip. "Better luck next time?"

"Yeah, I guess." I shrugged.

"My god, that's a shitty movie." he laughed.

"I can't believe I've seen it at all."

He assured me that he'd take me out again in the hopes of meeting an intelligent woman, but I had more doubts than ever.

***

My next 5 dates had the same conclusion. My suave, foreign speaking patterns caused the women to become enamored with me, but they all asked the same question: "Is every British movie as funny as Four Weddings and a Funeral?"

I could've been smart. I could have asked if every American film was like Bio-Dome. But the slight air of racism and stupidity in the question forced me to kill them. And yet, somehow I don't spend my days eating Nutri-Loaf and using cigarettes as currency. Society is asking for these seaweed-brained women to be done away with, so it seems.

I've decided to stay in America. My talents would be wasted at home.

The Next Page

By James Cotter

The woman, whose name is Dorothea, or maybe just Dorothy, knows this is the day he will stay with them. She holds her daughter's hand as they enter the restaurant. The entranceway has wood paneling, a large fountain gurgles and splashes, and a large vase of flowers sits to one side on a formal table. The hostess stands behind a mahogany podium.

"Mom, this is a fancy place."

Dorothy, or Dot, laughs and says, "It is, isn't it."

The little girl looks all around. The young hostess – why are all the hostesses so young these days? – greets them. "Table for two?"

"Three, I'm expecting someone," the mother says. The hostess reached for three menus. "Oh, excuse me," the mother says, "I forgot to mention that he says to sit by the window."

The hostess nods and they follow her to a window front table. The windows line the whole wall of the restaurant and reveal a lovely view of the river. It is early in the day and there are only a few other people in the restaurant.

"Can I get you like something while you're waiting?"

"Do you have Mr. Pibb?" the daughter says. "It's my favorite."

"Dr. Pepper?"

"Oh, that's all right."

"And I'll have tea," Dot says.

Out the window, they watch the boats go by on the river. The river flows wide and full. "Where does the river start, Mommy?"

"A long way away, dear, way up in the mountains in tiny streams which come down the mountains."

"Why does it come here, I mean, this way, and end up here?"

The mother, Dot, laughs. "I'm sure I don't know. I never even thought of that question. It's just the way it comes over the land." She points out different sights to the little girl. She talks about the boats and, when she has pretty much exhausted what she has to say about the river, she pulls out crayons and paper from her large, black purse and hands them to the little girl.

"Is he coming soon?"

"Very soon, dear."

What came were their drinks. "Hi there," the waitress says. "You're a cutie. I love that curly red hair. I'm Carol and I'll be your waitress. A Dr. Pepper for the little girl and here's your tea." She sets the drinks down. "Do you want anything while you're waiting? an appetizer?"

Dot had not even looked at the menu. "Do you have chicken strips or something like that as an appetizer?"

The waitress nods and takes out her order book. "One order of the Captain's chicken fingers. That it for now?"

"Yes, that's all." Dot puts her tea bag into the water. She hopes Harold will come soon. She likes him very much. She feels better since he has come into her life. He is good for her and he is good with Lily. She knows that from the last time when he first met Lily and liked her. She is a bit of a standoff child, especially with men. Understandable with all those women around her all the time – Aunt Selma, Mother, Natalie and the rest of Dot's friends. Lily has spent most of her time so far with them. Dot thinks of herself as a bit awkward with men too. It isn't like she had spent a lot of time around men, other than the occasional short-term relationship. Not since Lily was born and that was getting to be a while ago in her story.

She places the cloth napkin on her lap. She wore her olive pants, her best ones, the ones that showed off her butt so well. And her little lime-green chemise that she felt so good wearing and over it all the light sweater Aunt Selma had given her. It was so old that some of the sequins on the shoulders are coming off but she loves the way it looks and the fact that it was Aunt Selma's. All in all, she feels she looks quite lovely. Robert had cut her hair last week and it hung down her back in layered waves of auburn.

She will stand up when he arrives she decides. She will stand up and embrace him when he comes in. She looks so lovely and so expectant that he will stay with her.

The river sparkled, or perhaps twinkled, in the late morning sun. Dot sips her tea, and when she looks out the window again, he is there. She has not noticed the dock before, but there it is and there he is. He steps off a small cabin cruiser, walks to the end of the dock and looks up toward the windows. He waves. She is unsure how he can see her, but she waves back. He walks quickly down the dock toward the restaurant. At the end he pauses and waves again like a figure in some old home movie.

He is handsome. His eyes are always his best feature. She likes blue eyes best. He wears a boater and a loose fitting blue shirt and tan linen pants, pleated and cuffed. They hang just right on him. He is a fit man with a spring to his walk. She likes that too. She wants a man with energy, good energy, to enliven her. And she needs a lover. Harold could become that for her. She looks at Lily. Her child needs a father or at least a male figure in her life. It's important.

Yes, she will rise and greet him when he comes in. She wants to embrace him and hold her to him, not let him go. She knows he will feel the same. He will be so glad to see her and to be here.

Dot takes another sip of tea and puts the napkin on the table, a blue napkin on a white tablecloth. Her daughter concentrates on drawing. She is filling the page with her coloring. Dot turns in the chair, ready to rise.

She sees him come in and the young hostess – why are they all so young? – greets the man – Harold was his name last time – and points to Dot and the little girl. He nods, turns to them, waves again and comes across the floor. Dot is so excited that she will be with him again.

As she begins to rise from the chair, he stops midway across the restaurant. She sinks back down and holds a hope but knows he is not coming over. He just stands there frozen, one leg stretched for a step, smiling. She can not see his eyes well but they look brown. She sits back down in her chair and puts her napkin on her lap again.

"Why isn't he coming over, mommy?"

"I guess he isn't right yet, dear." She looks out the window. The dock is gone and when she looks back, the man is gone too.

"What happened to him?"

"Our author decided to discard the man and start again. I think he's torn the page out of his notebook and is starting on the man again or maybe he's given up for the day."

"Will he throw us away too?"

"I don't think so. I think he likes us, what he's done with us so I think he'll only throw away Harold and he's on the next page," the mother says.

"Don't be sad, mommy."

"Oh, I'm really not, darling. There will be another Harold. There always is. He'll get it right, he always does."

The little girl nods. "Do you think he'd let me have the page he throws away? I can turn the sheet of paper over and color on it."

"I'm sure that will be fine, honey. It's our story after all."

Apostate Blues

By Jordan Eudy

I sat there for quite a while, watching all the people walk past, sipping my tea. Some guy, pants dangling from the middle of his butt, shouted as he stomped past, and his fellow loper, similarly dressed, laughed loudly. This startled me a little bit, so I compensated by clutching the lump of keys in my pocket, and shifted in my seat to check that my wallet was secure. A fine pair of legs tip-toed by on a set of brittle heels. She had a decent figure, but her face seemed stretched, and her puffy lips stuck out like an over-ripened fruit on a barren plain. Nevertheless, I watched the show come and go. I examined my watch again.

I went there early; not for her, but because I had some thinking to do. So when seven o'clock came and went, and she was late, I didn't mind.

Meanwhile, the speaker above me played that song from a movie I couldn't place. Light from the setting sun cast arched and fuzzy shadows across the top of the building, leaving jagged points of light along the stucco. The coffee shop door opened every so often, and the chill of air-conditioning came with it. Real glass ash trays-some filthy, some unused-sat in clumps like lily pads on the tables. A few people were huddled around them, smoking their ultra light cigarettes with cool satisfaction. All of them, first- and second-handers, were clutching their favorite blends of multi-syllabled delight. None for me thanks, just tea.

A car pulled into the lot, fan belt wailing in protest, and, for a moment, I thought it was her. But it wasn't. A weed-addled teen stumbled out instead, mainstream punk spilling after him. He got about halfway to the door when he realized that he'd left his car on. This kid, who had been driving a few seconds ago, just stood there, apparently deciding between coffee and car. I guess he figured that he could have both: weaving but determined, he managed to kill the engine, shut the door, and find the entrance again. Making a mental note to separate our departures by a healthy amount of time, I examined my watch once more.

She had called me the night before and told me she had something to say, but not over the phone. I knew that this could be one of two things: either she was pregnant or she wanted to break up. Whatever.

A young couple sitting a few yards away were making eyes at each other and playing footsie under the table. The textbook before them lay open and forgotten. The breeze played with the pages and I saw a pie chart flit into view and disappear. I think I might've looked at the book more than either of them that evening.

Suddenly, she was standing in front of me, her eyes bleary and her face free of makeup, looking positively gorgeous. She didn't look angry. Or pregnant.

"Hey."

"Hi," she said. Her gaze wasn't meeting mine.

"I'm gonna get something. Want anything?" she asked. I smiled and picked up my tea. She tried to smile back, but it showed up more like a grimace, and walked inside. I wanted to feel distracted, so I glanced at my watch again, a pastime which gave me no comfort now.

In the seat just beyond the love-struck students, that stoned teenager had set up shop, cradling a beaten guitar. Despite the palpable drug haze, he was pretty good. He hadn't come here to pick up girls; he was playing the blues. My mind drifted away to those old songs, grating a popping on the record player. My grandfather loved that music.

***

When I was a kid, I had always enjoyed visiting the boonies of Kentucky, where my grandparents lived. Usual fair: cookies and milk, stories that always hit the imagination in black and white, and the disappearance of bedtime. But what I remember best was the hour or so after dinner when-my stomach bulging with the extra piece of cake Grandma would always let me have-Grandpa would drag out his old six-string. From Leadbelly to Woody Guthrie to the stuff that grandpa had written himself; I loved it all. I was too young to understand what the words meant-the beauty of rambling across the country, the sorrow that grew in the Dust Bowl-but it didn't matter. It was the sound that captivated me. The way it would growl out of the wooden frame, carrying a feeling that went beyond words. Even as a child I could hear the weight of the world being played on those strings. Grandpa heard it too.

He had spent his younger days working in a factory-the class-typical 9 to 5 during his time-and his younger nights playing in local bars. That's how he met Grandma. She bussed tables and he played shows; eventually the got married. Again, usual fair: they both quit the night scene and found Jesus. But Grandpa never stopped playing music. He found a steady gig at the church they went to, playing hymns and other religious stuff, and continued his affair with blues and folk on the side.

Several children later, and a few grandkids after that, I showed up. By then he was, by any measure, a damn good guitarist. I think that's how it works: the people who are the best at what they do go virtually unknown for their entire lives, and fade away with the same amount of prominence under their belts. I was lucky enough to get to know this man, to learn to play from a real master.

But I grew older, and things changed. I watched him age, as diabetes tore away at his fingers, at his happiness. With his ability to play, went his faith. God became a guy who snatched his music away. Grandpa didn't like that, so he took his business elsewhere. And, eventually, God retaliated in fashion.

I thought about what he said that night, while grandma watched her TBN special-probably hoping desperately that one of those televangelists would recapture my grandfather's soul-and the dusty, out-of-tune guitar sat in the corner. He told me that if everyone was the same, life would be predictable and understandable, but so boring that no one would care. "That's why you've got to find what you're good at," he said, "what you love, and go after it with everything you got until the day you die, because that's all you have to make you stand out from the rest." On that day, I got his guitar.

So now I'm an insurance agent.

***

She came back with a cup of coffee and eased down into a chair, almost tentatively, like it was a new experience for her. Those big, green eyes kept bouncing around, never looking into my own. I don't know how long we sat there, drinking often to make an excuse for the lack of conversation. Presently, I ran out of tea, so I resumed my old standby of checking the time. I finally caught myself staring at my watch.

"So, what's up?" I asked.

"Nothing important. I just got off a helluvah shift. Pretty much spent the day getting yelled at by every customer."

"That bad, huh?" I tried to sound concerned.

"Yeah. I was this close to quitting on the spot,"-she raised her hand and held her fingers about an inch apart- "but I pulled through."

"Good work."

"How was your day?"

"Decent enough. I managed to sell a policy, but other than that, same old same old." I said. She fell silent again and I wished I had more tea.

I had lied for convenience's sake. The truth was more interesting, but I was distracted by my own thoughts.

***

Earlier that day, my boss's boss had stopped by my cubicle to have a word. It turned out that a pretty big potential client was coming in, and the agent that was supposed to court this giant had gone missing the night before (this isn't common, but it happens more than you'd think: insurance has a less glamorous postal side). My job, at the time, was to pick up the smaller accounts that the top agents didn't want. The biggest one I had gotten so far was worth about 500 thousand, but this new assignment blew that record out of the water. Six million. More money than I would ever see in my life. I got a quick profile of the client, got the typical 'you can do this' pep-talk, and he left me with a thick folder and a paternal-looking smile. Shit.

I thumbed through the pages quickly and saw that the meeting was in two hours. The guy's name was Dean Marsh, and he wanted to insure a basement full of expensive instruments and rare records. The spreadsheet for the pricing was already there, as was the finished contract. I sighed and felt a little less nervous.

Noon came and I headed down to the lobby to meet Mr. Marsh. He was younger than I had imagined, but his demeanor added about ten years. Tall and fair, his long face produced a casual smile when I approached him. We shook hands and exchanged pleasantries and I invited him up to the fifth floor conference room. When we sat down in the large, empty room, things started off poorly.

"So, what's happened to Mr. Lorrin?" he asked.

"Ah, well," I scrambled, "he's, um, very ill at the moment. I'm his representative; more of an assistant, really. I take care of his accounts when he can't."

"Or when he doesn't want to?" Marsh prodded, but with a friendly grin that set me at ease.

"Of course not," I replied, feeling more confident, "You're an extremely valuable and important client. We wouldn't dream of doing less than our absolute best for you."

"Potential client," he reminded.

With that, I launched into the official selling spiel. I got more comfortable as I worked through the numbers with him, going over handling contingencies, projected inflation indexes, and other business epithets for "more money." I was surprised by how much he understood, bringing up questions that only a well informed person would think to ask. Most of the people that I had dealt with only possessed a faint clue about insurance. But this guy was sharp.

When I was done, I leaned back in my chair, trying to conceal how smug I felt. He tilted back as well, and his face drooped in a slight frown.

"I don't know if I like the final price."

Damn.

"Well, Mr. Marsh, as you can see, all the cost have been assessed, and the final price, I think, is the lowest we can offer you," I said.

Brows still furrowed, he said, "That's a sizable chunk of change. I'll have to think about it."

I was getting desperate, so I went back to the numbers. He waved me off. "Look, you seem like a good guy, and you definitely know what you're talking about, but I know that you're trying to get this thing signed and sealed as fast as possible. Just give me a few days, and I'll get back to you."

"If you don't mind, Mr. Marsh, I'd like to say one last thing," I asked.

He sighed a little and nodded. I don't know what I was thinking, but I went for a new approach.

"It's obvious that you love music, Mr. Marsh. Otherwise, you wouldn't have all of these priceless reminders. I also have a soft spot for music, and, to be honest," I added jokingly, "I'm kind of upset that our meeting didn't take place in your home. I bet you have some records that I would give my right arm to listen to."

His face relaxed into a glowing smile. I continued, "And it's also obvious that you would find it unbearable to lose just one of these reminders. That's why you would even consider paying such an admittedly large (though, again, I believe fair) amount. I would do the same thing if I were in your place.

"People like us, Mr. Marsh, are often misunderstood by those that don't truly enjoy music. They don't see the sense in buying archaic records or ancient guitars. They think it's just nostalgia. They can't see the beauty of it, the incredible power of the things that remind us of the people who dedicated their lives to the pursuit of the perfect sound; those things that can lift us to the highest peak, or commiserate with our most intimate sorrow.

"But we see it, Mr. Marsh. We know the nature of these things. And that's what I can offer you. I ask that you not just consider this as a preparative, but as a relationship with someone who knows the true value of what you love, what you simply can't live without. And I think that's more than any other company can offer you."

I was sitting in my cubicle an hour later, after I had dropped the signed contract off at processing, staring at the grey carpet divider, trying to realize what had just happened. The Vice President of Customer Relations dropped by in person to congratulate me on a job well done. Words like 'promotion' and 'raise' were tossed around, but I wasn't really listening. I just nodded and said things like 'yes, sir' 'thank you, sir.' He clapped me on the back and left. Upper management must take courses in paternal smiles, because I got the same one that the other boss had given me. I sat there for the rest of the day, thinking about what I had said.

***

"What?"

"What are you thinking about?" she repeated, pouting.

"Nothing," I summarized.

There was an awkward pause that always follows such exchanges. She drank some more coffee, and I propped my tea back against my lips, forgetting that it was empty. I feigned drinking the last dregs and got up to throw the cup away. Between sitting and standing, she pronounced, "I think we should break up."

I sat back down. She was looking directly into my eyes, a faint curve of her lip betraying an insuperable resolution. The drugged-out guitarist nestled in his corner broke a string and cursed loudly.

"Alright," I said flatly.

She gaped. "Oh, um, okay."

"Alright," I said again.

"So," she stuttered, looking both hurt and surprised, "you don't really care?"

"Not really. Sorry." Men always share their emotions at the wrong time. Little diamonds began to form in the emerald settings. I went over to the trash can and left my contribution. Stopping by our table on the way to my car, I said goodbye.

"Wait, where are you going?" she asked. Her tone was almost begging. I smiled and brushed the hair from her face.

"Where I should have been all along."

And I walked away, humming the blues, happier than I'd ever been before.

October Nigh

By James Bowler

The call of the crow signals their time; it signifies the moment that you should be locked away inside. Doors closed, windows latched, fires burning bright and everlasting. Their month begins, and our time of hiding starts.

September 29th, only a day stands between their time and us. My newlywed wife and I rush around the store, amidst hundreds of other hurried customers, in an attempt to finish everything before the stores close tomorrow for the month. I try not to remember last October, our neighbors had left one of their windows open. I can still hear the crashing, and the screaming. I can still hear them calling for someone to help. No one dared though, no one was brave enough to face them; there was no might in the world that could face them. We just huddled and listened; there was nothing we could do but listen, as they slowly died.

My mind reacts quickly to an oncoming shopping cart. I try to maneuver out of the way but it's too late, and we crash carts, sending both of them tilting either way. Neither my wife nor I exchange words with the other couple. We simply put our things back in our cart and leave them to clear up their own matters. That is life before October, you think and react for yourself; you help no one but yourself. It's the only way to stay alive, to survive.

We finish grabbing everything we will need to last the month; mostly non-perishable items and frozen stock. Nothing fresh; nothing that will go bad. We need it to last us an entire month. As we rush to the checkout, my wife's grip tight and fast on my arm, I watch as a stock boy simply pours dozens of boxes of crackers into the isle; no longer bothering to carefully shelf each item. In moments, the crackers dwindle to less then a dozen boxes. The people are like crows to a dead carcass; they dive in and leave little behind.

As we leave the store, we watch as the parking lot is boxed in by dozens of cars trying to leave, the roads are not much better. I shoot a look at my wife, the look telling her it's going to be a few hours before we make it home. It's a good thing we brought the coolers.

September 30th, the day of reckoning, the day of all preparation my wife is up before I am; she is cleaning everything. All the windows are open, letting in the last of the fresh air we'll breathe in a month. I wake up to the sound of her banging the rugs against the wall outside.

I grab some slacks and prepare to get to work. I have no thoughts of showering or the time to do it anyways. It is time to work, to prepare, to be ready. As I'm heading outside to begin checking the roof, my boss calls. He gives me his and his wife's best wishes and says he hopes to see me in a month. I tell him the same, keeping our conversation short and curt. We both realize that there is not much to be done and little time for chitchat.

My work on the roof is quick; it's a new house and there are no holes or damaged roofing tiles to be found. Good news for me, and I throw a sorry sidelong glance at the new neighbors as they hurry to fix their patchwork of a roof. They really should have done it months ago, I think.

As I come down the ladder, I see my wife clearing weeds and dead brush from the garden I ask her why she is wasting her time with it, and she curtly tells me that even though there will be no one around to see it, that doesn't mean it needs to look like this. I tell her there is no time for such nonsense, but having none of it, she waves me away and quickly goes back to work. I shake my head, but know better then to argue with her. She needs a project to keep her mind off of what is coming anyways; as do I.

Soon, everything is done, and we have closed and latched all the windows. A healthy stock of woodpile is in the attached garage, more than enough to keep us going for a year. We don't lock the door yet, savoring the last moments of freedom that we have.

My wife flicks on the television while she makes dinner. The news announcer tells us that a small skeleton staff will be locked up tight in only this station's building for the duration of the month to bring us some form of entertainment; only repeats, but still, it will be something. I try not to think what might happen if the building isn't secured properly, the risk those people would be taking. I can't fathom being away from my wife for this month, this harsh time.

We eat dinner outside, enjoying the last time, we'll be able to do it for a while, and my wife turns on some music as we wordlessly shovel food into our mouths. Overhead, clouds begin to roll in; they will cover the skies for the month to come, as though brought there by them. A crow call makes me drop the glass I'm drinking from and it shatters on the deck. My wife gives me an annoyed look, and I, in turn, give her an apologetic one. We both know that the real calls begin later on, that this is just a fluke, and we should not take it as anything more. Still, we eat a little more hurriedly and then rush inside, not bothering to sweep up the broken glass; I'll get to it in November, I think.

11:59 PM, one minute before October the 1st. My wife is cuddled close to me but we are both awake. We are not able to sleep through this moment; I doubt that anyone would be. As the clock slips over to 12:00 AM, silence suddenly dawns the outside world. The crickets and other night animals fall deathly silent. It is then that the first caw begins. Seconds later, more crow caws join the first, then more. Before long, there are hundreds, possibly thousands of crows cawing at the same time; calling out, calling to their masters to start their time. Within five minutes, the cawing stops abruptly. Not a second past five minutes after twelve do they cry.

Then the banging starts, every door in every home, in every city. They all are hammered on, as if thousands upon millions of visitors seek refuge. We all know better though, we've become wise to it. It is their calling card. They beckon for an unlucky person to let them in They cannot open a door or a window; they cannot enter a home unless there is an entrance already opened for them

My wife suddenly grabs me by the scruff of my shirt and pulls on me. She asks if I remembered to lock the door; my mind searches but I can't remember the moment I did. I calmly hold her back and tell her that I'm sure I did, but to wait while I check. She cowers under the sheets as I move out of bed and into the hallway. The banging continues, it will go on like this for some time.

I flick the downstairs hall light on, and, as if propelled by this, the banging on our door grows louder and more insistent. It's as if the being behind the door believes I will be foolish enough to open it. My stomach tightens as I realize, I have not bolted the door, only locked the handle.

In an effort to keep a calm mind, I slowly make my way down the stairs and to the door. There is a bold glass window facing the outside world, my wife's choice; when she saw it she had to have it. Now I regret her decision, as I will have to look outside when I get closer to the door. Worse still, whatever is outside will get to have a look at me.

As I reach the door, the banging mysteriously stops. A chill runs down my spine and brings the hairs to full erect attention on the back of my neck. I have never experienced this before. The being can obviously see me now and is watching my every move. Slowly but surely, I reach for the bolt and grip it tightly. Suddenly, there is a slam against the door, louder than the others, and I jump back.

It slams again, as if trying to break the door down. I don't hesitate, but dive forward and click the bolt in the lock. There is a shrill cry from outside and a hiss, and then silence. I lean my sweat-covered forehead against the cool pane of the glass and sigh in relief. Outside, I hear the banging begin to die off on other doors as well until finally, it stops altogether.

They have given up, for now.

October 5th, and we still haven't been able to get used to the silence, the lack of cars, people, anything. They kept it all away; they destroyed any life other then those crows, which occasionally caw and cackle from time to time. My wife and I played Parcheesi today but I wasn't particularly good at it so I eventually stopped playing and went to the television. Indeed, so far the station in question has kept their promise of keeping the shows running, even if they are just reruns.

We're running electricity from a gas generator in the garage; I had managed to shimmy up a type of chimney for the fumes to expel from, rather than leaking back into our home and poisoning us. I assured my wife at the time that it would be safe and they wouldn't get in that way; I'm not sure if I believed it then or now. They are meticulous and will find any way to get into a home, any way at all.

Still, I don't think about it as I try to laugh at the sitcom playing on the TV. My wife also shares my attempts at joviality but it's hard considering what's just outside, what can come crawling up in seconds if we even open the door. We've tried to have sex the last few nights, we managed to do it a couple times a day when we were first married; but, she and I both know we're only doing it now to keep our minds off of what is happening around us; it takes away from the romance.

There's been little commotion outside, and we haven't seen our neighbors at their windows when we take an hour a day just to look outside at the world; it keeps us sane.

October 13th, and it's a Friday, figure that out. We're standing at the window looking outside the way we promised ourselves we would for an hour each day. It's cloudy, like it is everyday. Sometimes it even rains, but never worse than that. However, the wind has been pretty violent lately, hitting the house with gale force at times. We're holding each other, watching the street, when suddenly a small boy appears in a yellow raincoat. He's walking slowly, playing in the puddles that have accumulated.

My wife gasps but I keep her held close to me; we've both seen this trick before. It's a lure, trying to get us outside, to help the innocent little boy. We watch and hope that none of our neighbors have fallen for the trick, especially the new ones next door; we'd hate to lose those neighbors again.

Someone does come outside, but it's not the next-door neighbors. It's the old Italian lady from across the road. We can even see her old husband yelling at her to get back inside, but she doesn't listen. My wife buries her face into my chest, not wanting to see anymore, knowing what comes next. But, I can't seem to look away.

I watch as she reaches the boy, and as I expected, he disappears into dust. The attack comes quickly, black forms whiz past my peripheral vision, and not wanting to see anymore as well, I look away. We can both hear her terrorized screams, until she's ripped to shreds.

We don't expect the next screams we hear, but they appear to be those of her husband, who tried to go out to save his wife. I wonder if I would have done the same thing, as he is quickly torn apart as well.

We both look back at the road, which is now bathed in a thick layer of blood, but nothing more is left. Crows; just like crows.

October 25th, my wife and I have given up on having sex a week ago. It just seems too foul now to pleasure ourselves amidst such horror.

She did, however, start her baking phase; just something she gets into near the end, she's been talking to herself about the ingredients she's been putting in the muffins and such. I'm wondering if maybe there's something wrong with that, because she's never done it before.

I'm out in the garage today stock-piling some wood into the wood cubby that we keep near the fire so we won't have to continually keep running out into the freezing space to grab more. I fill it and then go to check the generator, just to make sure there's nothing wrong with the gauges or the gas flow I've hooked up a large 20-gallon tank to it, which I fill with gas, so I can keep it running continually without having to fill it up constantly.

I notice that there is a small smell of fumes in the area and I look around my makeshift chimney, made up of an old piping unit that I used for the air conditioner. There doesn't appear to be any problems near the unit, but when I get to the wall where it expels the fumes, I smell it a little stronger. I notice a small hole, possibly a tear in the seal between the wall and the pipe. It's probably from the acrid smoke, so I simply stick some duct tape on the hole. We're only a week away from the end of the month anyways, so I don't think too much of it.

October 29th, with only two days to go. Although, we're both on edge now. Yesterday, my wife and I got into a ridiculous fight and I nearly went outside, without thinking, to cool my head. My wife cried for hours after that, knowing she'd feel completely responsible if I had been taken. We've both seen a lot of things, things that would pull a weak-minded person out into the open. As well as many horrific things, it's starting to make us come apart at the seams

There's so much blood on the road, the rain is having a terrible time washing it away. There's also a head now too, the older gentleman from next door; they left it there to stare at us, to make us crazy.

I'm really starting to get sick of eating rice.

Halloween, the last night, thank God, though I don't understand how He can allow such creatures on us in the first place. It seems the new neighbors were smarter than the last. We haven't heard a peep from next door. I'm quite sure now everyone has seen the head in the road. I'll have to go pick it up tomorrow, as well as that broken glass on the deck.

My wife is no longer talking to me; I told her that the food was becoming unbearable; she threw the plate at my head and just missed. She then ran off crying, and hasn't talked to me since.

I'm in the garage now, gathering the last of what we'll need for wood, and I notice something. The gas smell is back, but this time it's much stronger. I move over to the wall where I've put the pipe through the hole, but to my utter horror, I find that the pipe has come completely loose of the wall and there is now a gaping hole to the outside world.

Without a second thought I grab the wood and move into the house, securely shutting the door and locking the handle. I wish we had put a bolt on this door, but I know that they will never be able to get in, even without a lock.

I begin to grow suspicious of how the pipe came loose; they couldn't have done it, they don't have the power to move objects and make entryways. I wonder if my seething wife, in the rage of last night, went in and saw that I had duct taped it. Maybe she thought she could give me a good scare. Wouldn't she be regretful if they had gotten in while I was there and killed me; wouldn't she be upset then…

I feel the rage start to build inside of me. Maybe I should give her a scare, a real good one at that. I hear things start to move around in the garage.

Midnight. In folk lore, "All Hallow's Eve" didn't end until day break; maybe that's why they don't leave until the sun begins to rise. Whatever the case, it is now November, but we must wait for the sun for our salvation to come once again.

They do their worst at a night like this; young children walk the streets in spooky and cute costumes, knocking at our doors, calling out "trick-or-treat." We know better, we all know better; and luckily for everyone, not a neighbor has strayed tonight; no screams visit us in the darkness.

It's now close to morning and we've been awake the entire time, my wife constantly baking everything she can find the ingredients for. I call for her; I'm going to get her back for her little prank. As she enters the back room, I tell her that I'm going to go get some wood to keep the fire burning until morning. I know she'll try to stop me when she realizes that, because of her sabotage, they are probably inside the garage now.

But, as she walks in and I start to open the door, she just stares at me expectantly; this makes me angry. Is she actually going to let me go through with this and play dumb? Does she think that this is going to be funny after they tear me to shreds? In a rage, I fling the door open and turn the light on.

Shadows scatter everywhere at once; they don't like the harsh light, hence why they call upon the rain during their month. They hide and screech at me. My wife's face turns from expectant to horrified. Now I see, now she is regretting her little prank, now she will fully regret it.

Suddenly the screeching grows louder and louder until I have to cover my ears. The sound breaks the glass bulb, showering the garage into darkness.

I am suddenly in utter shock and can't move. My wife begins to scream for me to close the door. I can hear them moving around, knocking over anything in their way. I feel a grip on my arm and, before I know it, I'm pulled into the darkness. I scream; all I can hear are the screeches of the creatures and my wife's distant screams.

I feel a sharp pain on my arm, and realize they have cut me deep. Suddenly, a bright light dances across the room and right into my eyes. They fly away again, frightened of the burning light. I look towards the source. My wife has brought our flashlight with her; she carries the damn thing everywhere.

She calls for me to come out, and I get up without hesitation, running forward. Although, before I can make it to the door, it's slammed shut in and I'm knocked down again.

It's now completely pitch black; I can hear the scuffling and breathing of them. One of them, however, makes a wrong movement and I hear a crack as the wall holding up my well placed wall of logs breaks and the pile comes cascading down. I can't see any of the logs but do my best to avoid them. One or two manage to hit me on my arm and leg, and I feel the sharp pain fly through those areas.

I struggle forward still, blindly, reaching for the handle. I feel the cold metal suddenly, and I yank the door open. My wife stands there with the flashlight held back in swinging position, ready to strike. She drops the flashlight and grabs me when she sees me. I, in turn, grab the handle, and yank the door behind me, but before I can fully close it, it jams.

I turn around and my eyes fall on the source of the jam; a small log has wedged itself between the floor and the door. I kick it out and try to close the door but there is something pulling now. They're behind the door, pulling, trying to get in; I feel their presence getting closer. They're going to get in and tear us to shreds, we can't stop them.

It's then that we hear the distant sound of bells; long, drawn out monotonous drones of bells. It's morning; morning has come. With one final desperate attempt, I pull the door and it slips from them and slams shut.

The bells continue to play their haunting tune; I fall backwards and stare at the ceiling, finally realizing the throbbing in my leg and arm, from where the logs have hit me. My wife is dabbing at the cut on my arm as well. It's not deep; it could have been a lot worse.

The bells continue and the scuffling and screeching in the garage begins to die down and then altogether dies out until there is no sound left behind at all. I look at my wife, we smile at each other and then she reaches down and kisses me deeply, all the while cradling my head in her lap.

November 1st, the new day of the new month; our lives can begin again. Life goes back to normal today, and as I clean up the broken glass from the deck outside, I look at the morning sun beginning to rise in the sky. The rain clouds are almost a distant memory as they slide away into the horizon.

As I finish sweeping and dump the glass in the trashcan, I'm suddenly disturbed by a loud noise behind me. It's a large black crow that has landed on the fence. It stares at me with its deep black eyes that never blink, never looks away I know what that stare means and I take it to heart; you may not be so lucky next year.

I shoo the crow with the broom and, as it caws angrily at me and flaps away, I move back inside. I may have the freedom to be outside once more, but nothing beats the comfort and safety of being indoors.

Articles

Your Diner

By Grant J. Bergland

You know the place.

It is a vintage diner with stainless steel on the walls, bright red vinyl booths, and a percolating jukebox. Or it has cracked leather seats, patched with spider webs of duct tape and laminated menus with prices whited out and redrawn with unsteady lines. It is in a bustling city with people marching outside like frenzied ants. It is alone by the side of the road as if the highway gave birth to it. It is a diner in the east that serves scrapple, or in the west with a breakfast burrito, in New England with fried clams any time of day, or in the south with grits and gravy.

Wherever it is, every diner has a counter. That's what makes it a diner and not a restaurant.

You can sit alone there. Diners are made for eating by yourself, they serve you with no questions asked- there's no "are you waiting for someone?" or "let me get this extra place setting out of the way." Nope. Without a word the waitress turns over your coffee cup and fills it. You remember how you read somewhere that the oldest diners were born outside of twenty-four hour factories to give workers a place to eat regardless of the time. The counter grew up around a grill, a set of stools arranged in a loose rectangle. You look at the grill with heat rising from it in waves and see it is still the case.

Many diners serve lunch, but you don't know too much about that side of the menu. Your eyes read the italicized words Breakfast Served All Day then glide over the menu without reading it. You imagine perfect pancakes coming soon like whispered promises. The griddle will fry the skins of the 'cakes toast brown, making a light crunch as you taste the butter, the baking powder, the flour, and the sweet, sweet syrup.

You ponder the holy trinity of the diner breakfast: eggs, bacon, pancakes.

Eggs make Denver omelets that snap with fresh bell pepper and diced ham and onion. Or the eggs cover inch thick slices of Texas toast to make French toast powdered with sugar and served with a single red strawberry. Or you will have the eggs alone or with Tabasco sauce or if you are lucky, you'll reach for Cholula with the wooden cap.

Salty bacon, with a ribbon of grease, stays covered in its thin coat of fat like a pat of butter sliding along a hot skillet. The pork slides so fast to the back of your throat you have to slow yourself, immerse your mind in its taste. Patty sausage, link sausage, firm Canadian bacon, pork chops, and grilled ham are a chanting chorus of salt, fat, and sage. All of the side meats lie next to one another on the grill in rows, sizzling sunbathers.

Sudden heat sears the hotcakes and brings bubbles to the white surface and pop open like mouths uttering a single silent word. Some of them are wide as dinner plates, and you wonder how the cook is able to turn them before the spatula slices under them like a scythe. The pancake batter made fluffy with egg whites, buttermilk, and oil makes waffles that run down the sides of the round iron.

You take two pancakes, throw a sunny side up egg between them and hide the white like a card trick. Somewhere under the surface war happens and yellow blood drips out one side. You saw into a piece of sausage and make a shish kebab getting every flavor onto one fork and into one bite. The sage explodes with forte before it is quieted by the heavy baritone of the pancake, and the slick egg makes the coda.

Part of you wonders about cholesterol, LDL, and insulin levels, but then the waitress returns and warms up your half cup of coffee. You look at her in gratitude and flash a returned grin, she is your carney at the fair and you are going for a ride.

Half sized glasses of water sweat with condensation, ignored while you reach for cold juice or more hot coffee. Crisp toast is sopped with butter from a paintbrush, the edges hard girders holding the wet insides like pieces of a sail. Lozenge-sized plastic tubs of strawberry, boysenberry, and blackberry jam wait in a wire basket.

Wherever it is, whatever time of day, rain or shine, the people in the diner blend together like mannequins in a store window.

A loud family with a toddler uses the high chair that normally stands neglected in the corner, the guy in the Lion's club hat eats in a booth by himself and stares longingly at his reflection in the window, a young couple sits on the same side of booth looking into each other's eyes, and a man in a grey suit reads the business section folded into a rectangle neat as the rest of him.

Somewhere, everywhere in America, a server drops off the food and heads for the coffee pot with an open hand, the cook goes out for a butt, and someone else sits down at the counter. You set the fork down and leave the money by a bill scrawled out in an indecipherable hand. You don't know how much it is, but what you left is more than enough.

How to Win a Short Story Contest with a Dead Baby
By Michael G. McLaughlin

How to win a short story contest?

The obvious: No typos, spelling mistakes, faulty grammar, exotic and/or experimental styles like stories with no capital letters or a 13 page story as one run-on sentence. Gratuitous use of the words: "fuck" "shit" "mother fucker" "cock sucker" "shag me till I'm dry" or "anal sex is fun with two hung chaps" will XXX you out of winning a story contest. You must always follow the rules as to format, i.e. double spacing, name/no name in the upper right corner, word count, etc, etc, etc. If the story contest length is between 3000 and 5000 words make it closer to 3000 words. Most stories, no make that ALL stories, can be made better by making them shorter. Unlike sex, in literature, shorter is better. Moby Dick would have been a better book 50 pages shorter. (That was not a double entrée cheap sex joke.)

Now let's get into the minds of the judges.

If you are a judge staring at a stack of 200 stories, 30 pages each, what are you going to do? Read every single word in every story and then contemplate the merits in a serene moment of literary clarity? Get bloody real! Judges are ruthless and lazy bastards. As soon as the reader experiences too many of above mistakes, or their eyes flutter in boredom you're in the trash bin. Why should they read a bad story all the way through? They don't.

If, for some reason your story is the 199th read out of 200, you won't win. By then the judges have reader fatigue. Sorry, but you can't control when your story will be read. You may be first or last. It's the luck of the draw. Life and contests are not fair. I suggest you turn in your story early because some of the contests read stories as they come in. Plus, if you are read late in the process, whatever theme you use has already been penned by other writers.

What, you think you can write a story that is so exceptional, creative, imaginative and one of a kind?

More fodder for thought:

Let's do some math boys and girls. Say, 100 stories are entered in a SMALL contest. (The larger ones have thousands) Figure that half (50) of the stories are shit (Can I use that word? What, I have already?) Another 10 are full of the above errors and lack luck or are damned by the Fates. Now you are competing with 40. Let's say you have a damn good story, better than half. Down to 20 contestants. Lose 10 more, just for the hell of it and now you are in the top ten. Divine Intervention and you are in the top five. If you finish 4th out of 100 you get squat. Wow, you might win "honorable mention." Anything but first is warm beer. You get cold pee soup. You get foreplay and no bang. If you do the math in entering a contest, well, don't, you will never win.

OK, some real help.

So what factors make a winning story? What is the most important factor to consider when submitting a story? Here is the part that you will never hear from the contests or judges. They have to deny this. What you write about is more important than how well you write. I recently did an unscientific survey of winning stories to discern if there was anything similar about THE winning entry. This is what I found. (If you don't believe me do your own research.) Two of first three winning stories I read had as their theme...a dead baby. Yes, the winning stories had dead babies! I'm not kidding. I'm dead serious. Most contests (except the humorous ones) have an unwritten code: Dead serious wins. And nothing is as serious or emotional as a dead baby story. In other words no matter how clever your story is, or how funny the story, it stands not a chance in hell, none, nada, zip of winning. OK, maybe a judge might have a sense of humor, but don't count on it. I'm sure there are humorous stories that do win; but like UFO sightings or crops circles there is damn little evidence. About like the chance of Vancouver wining the Stanley Cup. (That was a Canadian joke.)

Why does humor rarely win? Funny I should ask. Because two people can't agree on what is funny. Clever especially is looked upon as a gimmick. Example: This is funny... "Science has finally discovered why women fake orgasms... (Pause) Men fake foreplay."

Again for emphasis:

Dead baby stories trumps all. The good news is there are other themes that stand a good chance. Such as: A father's/mother's suicide.... A deteriorating relationship into insanity... A dead soldier and his pregnant wife suffering with flashbacks of ironic anguish... A loved one (especially the innocent) dying slowly of cancer is a good theme choice. Incest? Maybe. Sex with a child? No chance of winning there. But a dead baby is the best theme. Two dead babies are better. NOTE: The law of diminishing return says no more than two. Three dead babies in one story are bit over the edge. Four is ludicrous. Five is funny. Six dead babies in one story is a farce and a farce will never win any story contest. Also please note that A.I.D.S stories are passé. It still is a horrible killer but packs no punch in a literary sense—Might have won a story contest 25 years ago, but not today. Ditto for stories about dying rainforests, killing baby seals, baby whales or drowning baby kittens with your bare hands. Yes, there is a dead baby in those stories but it is an animal.

Differences between men and women judges.

Men and women are different. Duh, really? A tumultuous relationship story is a good theme if the judge is a woman. Believe me most women (judges) love relationship stories? Stories that ooze with raw emotion. They really REALLY do like these stories. A mother/daughter relationship story is great winning story for a woman judge. Many, no make that most, women have or had a rocky relationship with their mother and they can relate to that kind of story. I would enter the contest with a fake woman's name, like "Austina Jane." Clever, eh? A common criticism of female readers (and female judges) is male writers don't write realistic "women speech." Of course that is nonsense. A good story is NOT about a woman or a man, it is about a HUMAN and we are the same and all capable of any individual behavior, emotions or word choice.

A gritty war story or car chase scene with bloody, sucking chest wounds is not a woman's cup of meat. Actually the preceding is rarely liked by men judges either. Action/adventure stories never win too. Also, never make the butt of a joke nor bad person a woman character either. If there are two characters and one is an angel and other is a dirty rotten bastard....well, play it safe and vilify the guy. Political correctness is alive and well in the modern prose.

Flavors of judges.

Sometimes the judges are announced for the contest. Look them up and see what they have written. Judges have flavors like ice cream. They won't have any idea if you "sort of copy" their themes and write what they write about. A professor in an MFA program has a prejudice for an MFA type story. Don't know what that is? Basically it would be an atmosphere story that is flawlessly literate and ending in a calm Angst. There would never be an exclamation mark in the story. MFA writing programs regurgitate writers like a Thomas Kinkade painting—That is, the stories have great technique, beautiful, pretty prose, but lack something. If I had to put it into words (I am a writer) I would say their writing lacks guts, bravery and individuality. Pedantic judges (both sexes) believe that careful constructed prose and theme is a substitute for creative imagination…. Right now an editor is reading this with an MFE degree…hands twitching…about to cast my story into the slush pile of death. Yawn. I've been killed by better.

Let me belabor the point one more time.

It doesn't really matter how clever or creative your story is, subject matter and sad serious tone is what wins contests. Dead babies win!

A sad story is easy to write. Sorry, it just is. As someone said: Death is easy, comedy is hard. Just make your story sad, and we all know what that is. But we all don't now what funny is. In contests it is the triumph of sad stories (style) over all other writings.

Kill the baby and win.

Flash Fiction

Boxes

By Leigh Byrne

In my hazy half-sleep I can hear the shower running, smell the scent of Dial soap wafting from the bathroom. I slide my hand across to Marty's side of the bed and it feels cold. I'm afraid to open my eyes. Afraid the boxes are still there. If the boxes are still there then Marty is not in the shower.

Our first morning in the house I forgot the mattress was on the floor, and when I tried to get up to go for a run my feet smacked flat against cold hardwood.

Marty laughed. "Would it kill you to skip a day?" he asked. "We've got a lot of unpacking to do."

I wish I had. Skipped that day. But I couldn't. Not if I wanted to eat. "Good, you're awake, you can go with me," I said, patting him on the butt. "I'm not sure about the neighborhood yet."

Marty opened a box of his clothes, and we dug around until we found some sweats to wear, and then headed out for a short run. We stood on the front porch for a minute and took a long, proud look at our new house. It wasn't much-a two bedroom Cape Cod, a fixer-upper. But we'd both fallen in love with the charm of its imperfections.

"We ate a lot of Ramen noodles to get that house," Marty said, and we laughed.

As we ran down the long, sloping driveway, I made a mental note of a bare thorn bush under the picture window that had to go, and further out in the yard, a birdbath badly in need of a couple of coats of paint. When we came to the end of the drive, Marty got between the road and me. It reminded me of when we first started dating. Whenever I was in the car with him and he had to make a sudden stop, he flung a stiff arm in front of me so I wouldn't be thrown forward. Like my life was more important than his.

After five years of sleeping with Marty, my body was practiced in finding the rhythm of his. The thrust of my legs and arms, even my breathing joined his in perfect synchrony. We ran without talking. Our relationship had reached that comfortable place where there was no need to engage in idle conversation. Except for the occasional snap of brittle twigs, the steady pounding of our feet against the ground was unbroken, lulling my mind back to where it always ended up.

This is what I was thinking before it happened: I will burn around 225 calories running, so to appease Marty, I can eat a few bites of an egg white omelet for breakfast. But I'll have to put a little yoke in to make it appear yellow, like his. I'll break up my toast and push the food around on my plate in a way that makes it look like I've eaten more.

This is what I was thinking when it happened: How can I squeeze in extra exercise today without Marty knowing? Maybe I can jog in place whenever I go to the bathroom...

Freak accident. That's what everyone kept saying at the hospital, at the funeral. The accident: An old woman has a stroke on her way to church and runs off the road, and like a skilled butcher's cleaver separates good meat from fat, her car slices Marty from my side. The freak: The freak of the accident remains, unharmed. Only the best part of her has been lopped off, the one part that made her feel human.

The stacks of boxes, now dusty, still taped, their contents marked in bold black, loom tall around me in the dim, early morning light. They surround me, contain me. Like a tiny ballerina in a music box I wait for the lid to open. But even if it does, I can't get out, only twirl my skinny body around and around in an aimless circle, and then back in the box I go until my next performance.

I haven't run in over a week, not since it happened. There are hardly any calories in Diet Coke and saltines. Most days I lay on the mattress pretending it was our first morning in the house. In my fantasies we don't get up to run, instead, we make love, moving from room to room, and then we eat a huge breakfast. In my fantasies I eat heartily, without regret, like when I was a kid.

I get up and go into the kitchen, feeling light and wispy, like I'm made of paper. I open the refrigerator and assess its contents: a dozen eggs, an expired quart of milk, a package of cheese singles. I fold a piece of cheese between a slice of stiff bread and take a quick bite, like I've seen people do. The heft of the food is intrusive to my body, and I fight to get it down. The instant it drops like a bowling ball to the bottom of my stomach, I want it out again. I wonder what a fingernail scratching the back of my throat would feel like.

The days continue without Marty. Milk expires. Bread gets stale. People eat. They bathe. They brush their teeth and get dressed. I toss the sandwich in the trash and return to the bedroom. I pick up the box cutter from the dresser where he left it, and slide the blade down the taped groove of a box marked "Ashley's clothes"

Holy Liftoff

By Elaine Medline

Cynthia swung a screwdriver.

"What are you doing with that?" her mother asked her.

"Fixing Gemini."

Gemini was the name that Cynthia had given to her new bicycle, a Stingray Deluxe. The girl was thrilled with the glitter banana seat and monkey bars, but had wanted the copper color. All they had in stock was violet.

"What's wrong with Gemini?" Joan asked.

"It's purple, first of all," her daughter answered. "Plus I don't like the fenders and chain guard. I ripped them off for liftoff."

"Cynthia, it was your birthday present."

Her son, Thomas, shuffled into the kitchen backward. He asked her what she was doing.

"Beating egg whites for a pie," she said, proudly holding up her new kitchen tool, a wire whisk.

"Holy smell, what's this? Clue me in."

Holy this, holy that. Batman was taking over his little mind.

"With the crackers? Cheese."

"Cheese didn't smell before," he said, exiting backward. "And it used to be orange."

Joan could hear the serious voice of a newsman on their television in the next room. She didn't want Thomas or Cynthia to hear it, so she turned it off. The news started getting bad around 1961, and that was five years ago.

While Joan was trussing the chicken, Thomas returned to the kitchen, this time in a forward direction, upset and talking fast. "Cynthia says she's gonna ride her bike straight up the garage," he said. "All the kids are coming to watch."

"What do you mean, ride her bike up the garage?"

"Straight up the garage door," he answered. "All the way to the roof."

Joan panicked inside. It wasn't physically possible to ride right up a garage door. But she could understand why a person would try. She continued working on the chicken, tying knots, thinking.

"Well, aren't you going to stop her?" Thomas demanded. "She says she's going to do a wheelie, then pedal like crazy to the top."

Of course I'll have to stop her, Joan thought. Even if her daughter managed to gain the momentum to accomplish her ridiculous goal, she'd still have to fall. In fact, the more successful her launch, the harder her fall.

"When is she going to do it?" she asked her son.

"Soon, maybe now. Hurry, or she'll die."

Joan rinsed the grease off her hands and rushed to the living room, which had a view to the front. She lifted the windowpane. True enough, half the neighborhood youngsters had gathered on the street in a semi-circle. The children were clapping in unison and rhythmically shouting her daughter's name.

Opening her mouth to stop the spectacle, Joan changed her mind. She said nothing. She reasoned it out. If Cynthia didn't try riding her bike up the garage, the next escapade could be more ambitious. Cynthia had a wild air about her, as if she would one day take up the guitar, or dance naked at Berkeley. Children had to learn their lessons, painful as they were. Joan wondered how her husband John would handle this.

John's not here, he's away at war, he's not coming home anytime soon. Handle it yourself, she disciplined herself. She fetched the first aid kit. There would likely be blood, so she readied the bandages and iodine.

The children had stopped shouting. The air smelled like crab apples. A wind shook the tree in their front yard, and chestnuts lightly thudded the pavement. The chestnuts, they reminded Joan of the B-52 bombs. Cynthia walked her bike out to the middle of the street, and the kids parted to make way for her. Now facing the garage, she edged herself backward to get a better run of it.

She closed her eyes and pursed her lips. Her hands revved the grips like she was on a motorcycle. She lifted her left foot from the asphalt and set it on the pedal. Then she picked up her right foot and pedaled like the devil. Her body ascended from the bike seat. Her legs reeled. Her hair rose. Just before she hit the garage, she pulled up her front wheel.

And her mother watched, fascinated.

Vintage

By Patricia McCowan

Christine spots the suit towards the back of the dusky shop. No, the suit spots her. She has escaped her desk at the brokerage for an illicit lunch hour. She has taken a long walk away from the towers, found a street of little brick buildings and grime. Now, inside, Christine makes sure her cell is off, checks over her shoulder. Just the burgundy-haired girl at the counter, idly flipping through an old Life magazine. Christine stands in place, prolongs the moment, describes to herself what's caught her: Size Eight Ladies' Tailored Grey Suit, 1930's. Severe, somber. Her breathing slows, the musky smell of the place like a tranquilizer. She goes to it. She reaches out and pulls the garment towards her, strokes the pleasurably raspy fabric of the jacket and matching skirt. The sensation catching on her nerves like tiny hooks. She narrows her eyes, pauses like a swimmer on a sun-heated dock, then slides her hand inside the skirt. Lined, she knew it would be lined. The old silk a thin barrier against the scratchy wool. She splays her fingers against it.

Maybe she could have it. Maybe she has to have it. She could buy it and a few faded blouses, pack a small, hard suitcase with underwear and stockings to be hand-washed in a sink at night and dried over the foot of a metal bed. Yes.

She'd take that suitcase and board a stale bus to a town with a Main Street of stubby buildings, brush-cut architecture. Buildings with bulky, solid doors and short staircases. No elevators. Buildings with windows that can open, with blinds that can close. In that town, Christine would carry her hard suitcase off the bus and walk alone in black shoes down the street. Men might tip their hats to her, women pushing strollers might nod and smile, but no one would talk to her, no one would need anything from her.

She'd come to a lunch counter. Push open the watery-glassed door. Inside would be a fan up on the greasy ceiling, pushing the air around, and a few men along the counter, reading newspapers in their shirtsleeves, suit-jackets and fedoras on the stools beside them. There would be a woman and her stooped mother at a booth, each nursing their lemonades with chipped ice, not looking at each other. A ballgame no one seems to care about playing on the radio by the cash. No one here has discovered rushing yet.

Christine would put her suitcase into a booth, slide in beside it, and order a ham and swiss and a coffee from the waitress with the friendly look about her. Maybe she'd even get a slice of pie. Nobody's too skinny here, no one would judge her. The lunch would be satisfying but not filling, even with pie. There would never be too much of anything in this place, in these clothes.

She would pay her bill, putting paper money right into the waitress's hand and getting change back as coins in her hand, and putting those coins in a change purse with a hard clasp that shuts tight, and putting that change purse in her handbag. You know where you are with a handbag.

She'd go freshen up in the ladies' room, where a window looks out on garbage cans and a patch of dried-out grass with an empty teeter-totter on it. The children who played on that teeter-totter are gone, Christine would think, they're grandparents, or maybe even dead. Time ticks on.

No! No, she'd look hard at her face in the mirror, convince herself to stop thinking like that. Time is malleable. She'll powder her nose.

After, the counter girl will give her directions down the street and around the corner to the rooming house with the yellow front porch and a sparse row of marigolds huddled along the foundation. A short walk. Christine will go up the steps and knock on the quilted metal bottom of the door. She will peer through the screen to a narrow hallway, dark at one o'clock on a September day, and watch the landlady emerge from the kitchen at the back of the house and come towards the door, slowly, drying her hands on a well-used apron. Floor boards squeaking. Christine will be patient. She will put her trust in this woman.

She will live alone in a dull room upstairs, with a narrow bed and a dresser with the drawers lined in not-yet-yellowed newspapers, and eat meals cooked by the fat, frazzle-haired woman emerging from the dark innards of the unfamiliar house. She will know only this as her future. A life of cold solitude and lack. And she will be content. Finally.

Christine lets the suit fall from her hands and it swings back into its proper place on the rack. Looks around, blinking. The girl at the front is staring out the front window, finished with the magazine. Christine should get back to work now. Things, deals, people — they'll all be piling up. She pulls her cell phone out of her purse. Time is piling up. Christine stands very still.

Price Increase

By John Bruce

Digital Discipline Technologies, which everyone refers to by its abbreviation DDT, has, like most such places, a company cafeteria in its world headquarters building. It's proud of its cafeteria. It has a variety of ethnic foods, and it's been designed to give employees little alcoves where they can eat with a sense of privacy and thereby reduce the stress they build up while working at DDT. In fact, it's been cited as one of the factors that put DDT consistently on some list or other of the 200 best places to work.

"In these difficult economic times," said R. Bambi Presswell, Senior Vice President for Human Resources in a recent issue of DDT's house organ, The Digit, "we're especially concerned at holding the line on prices in the cafeteria. We feel we're working with our employees to maintain mutual trust and productivity in light of our recent adjustments in health and retirement benefits."

It goes without saying that those adjustments were downward. And whatever the employees saved on the enchilada casserole entrée would definitely not offset those adjustments to health and retirement benefits.

Bob Stiles generally ate the spaghetti and meatballs entrée every Tuesday. The meatballs in fact weren't bad. On one particular Tuesday though, something changed: the lady behind the counter ladled out sauce – thin, watery sauce – but no meatballs. "What happened?" asked Bob. "No meatballs?"

"No meatballs," the lady replied, shaking her head.

He double-checked the menu on the wall. The price for the spaghetti without meatballs was the same as the old price for spaghetti with them. "No meatballs, but the price is the same?" he asked. The lady nodded her head.

She'd already put the spaghetti on the plate and ladled the sauce over it, and she handed it over to him. "I don't want it," he said. "Take it back."

The lady shook her head again. "I've served it up," she said. "You asked for it. You have to take it."

"No way. I thought it had meatballs when I asked for it. Then I saw it didn't have meatballs, but you're charging the old price for meatballs."

"You still have to take it," the lady said. "You ordered it."

The discussion caught the cafeteria manager's eye, and she came over to talk to him. "You ordered the spaghetti entrée," she said. "What's the matter?"

"There used to be meatballs. . ."

She cut him off. "I heard what you were saying. The price is the same. There's been no price increase. If you don't want to take it, I'll just get your badge number, and we'll deduct it from your paycheck."

With that, he had no choice. He paid the cashier, took his tray to a table, and began to eat his lunch. Before long a woman sat down across from him. "I'm Tammy from Human Resources," she said. "Apparently there's a problem. What happened?" She had a pen and a pad of paper with her. "Can I see your badge, by the way?" He handed it over to her, and she wrote down his name and employee number.

"The spaghetti entrée used to have meatballs with it," he said. He pointed to the plate in front of him. "They've taken out the meatballs, but the price is still the same."

"Where's the problem?" asked Tammy. "There's been no price increase."

Bob tried to summon up material from the econ class he'd had years earlier. "If I used to sell four widgets for a buck, but now it's three for a buck, there's been a price increase."

"Mr. Stiles," she said talking slowly and carefully to him as though he were a child, "there's been no price increase. That example has nothing to do with the spaghetti entrée. The price of the spaghetti entrée is still the same."

He was going to say more, but he realized nothing he said would make any difference. "I guess you're right," he said. "Have a nice day."

"Er, you have a nice day, too," she answered, getting up. She looked warily back at him over her shoulder. Bob knew his boss was going to get a call from Tammy, something about making trouble in the cafeteria. A good boss would blow it off. On the other hand, his boss wasn't a good boss. One encounter like that wasn't enough for a write up – but he'd already found a way around that. He'd save up two or three and write him up for the whole bunch.

.

Micro Fiction

The Poem In Your Pocket

By John Ammirati

I am a jealous lover, and this morning I searched through the pockets of the trousers you left at my house, looking for any evidence of infidelity I could pin on you; I always enjoy grilling you with my suspicion, but when I found the poem in your pocket I felt a thrilling new anguish. It was a beautiful, anonymous poem entitled "Dear Robert". I was jealous not only because you have a secret admirer, but because he is a far better poet than I will ever be.

I tore apart my room in a rage after reading the poem; I cried; I re-read the poem. Then I plagiarized it, changed the title to "Dear Peter", and gave it to Peter Hoskin, my gym instructor. Flattered, he asked me out and we're going on a date this Friday.

Lunchtime

By Ian Lamberto

Surrounded by the foliage of fall, Charlie and Sarah sat on the only bench in the park still made of wood, the only one that still creaked and cracked when used. They liked the sounds, the way the aged pine reminded them of its presence, the warmth that it kept between its decade-old wrinkles. There was something reassuring about it, something gentle, something that helped sweeten the taste of the peanut butter and strawberry jam sandwiches that they shared.

It was their lunch hour. It was their tradition.

"Nice day today," said Charlie, as he always did.

"That it is," responded Sarah, as she always did.

"Busy in the office."

"The phones won't stop."

"Wouldn't be much work if they did."

"Suppose not."

A few moments passed. Birds chirped from above, making their own idle conversation. The trees, ruffled by a cool breeze, released a sampling of golden leaves to the air. And Charlie stared at his half-eaten sandwich resting idly upon its bag.

"I'm leaving," he stated.

"Okay, bit early though, isn't it?"

"That's not what I meant," Charlie's leg started to shake. "I'm leaving...tomorrow...for good...."

Sarah took a drink of water from her thermos; this new script was making her restless.

"You're joking?"

"I'm not."

"Where will you go?"

"Don't know."

"Don't know?"

"Don't know."

Sarah set her sandwich down, her appetite fading.

"Why?"

"Why what?"

"Why are you leaving? Is it the job?"

"No."

"Is it the city?"

"No."

"The weather?"

"No," Charlie lowered his head. "It's you...."

"Me?" Sarah looked stunned.

Charlie's mouth opened, dismay passed over his face.

"I'm...I'm sorry...it's just...," he stammered.

"Just what?"

"Well, everyday we sit here, right here, and eat our little lunch, and drink our little water, and say nothing...sure we talk, but we never say anything, and I cannot take it anymore."

Sarah's shock quickly gave way to anger.

"Wait, that came out wrong," Charlie raised his hands in defense. "I...I...."

"Yes?"

Charlie returned his gaze to the ground, his heart beating faster than ever before.

"I'm in love with you!" he blurted.

"You are...?" Sarah eyes widened, as her pulse caught up to his.

"Have been for quite a while now...."

"Why didn't you tell me before?"

"I don't know," Charlie shrugged. "I enjoy our time together, I really do...being here, even without the words...I guess I...I guess I didn't want to lose that...."

"But you're moving away."

"Well, um, about that...."

"That wasn't true, was it?"

"Afraid not."

"Already lying and we've only begun to date."

Charlie's face twisted in surprise.

"Date?"

"You hide love a lot better than you detect it," Sarah smiled.

"You mean...," for the first time Charlie saw what had been there all along.

And he took her hand, and he stared into her eyes, and she stared into his; and neither moved until the hour had ended.

Rorschark Attack

By John Wiswell

A Washington D.C. Rationalist Think Tank was on holiday at the undisclosed beach that day. Three employees saw it break the surface. Tammy saw a deck of playing cards. Guido saw a platter of fried shrimp. Ironically only one of the rationalists, Virginia Welsley, saw a shark fin. Even more ironically, she was the only rationalist in the water.

She swam like Hell. Tammy would attest that the shark went straight after Virginia, while Guido swears it swam in the opposite direction. Other beach-goers looked when they heard the screams, but the majority said they didn't see a shark at all (while three saw an ice cream truck treading water behind Virginia).

When Virginia looked over her shoulder mid-breaststroke, she saw the gaping jaws of her third grade Math teacher – the one who always put impossible bonus questions at the end of his quizzes, presumably just to watch his pupils struggle and fail. That pungent memory felt apt as she swam for her life, and even more apt when she was seized in the middle-aged Math teacher's overbite.

She was fortunate enough to awake, alive, in the local ICU. Apparently the shark had nearly ripped her in half. After much fighting with her doctors she was allowed to see the damage the shark had done to her torso. When the medical technician removed the bandages so that she could see the marks he instantly stepped back and crossed himself.

"It's the Blessed Mother!" he exclaimed, looking at the bizarre shape of her bite wounds. She frowned at him and looked down.

"No it isn't." she said disdainfully. Then she squinted at the sutures. "Is… is that a Ferris wheel?"

Schimmler

By Richard Grossman

It's been ten days. No desperate craving, no headaches, no obvious depression. Carole asked me earlier why I'd quit smoking.

General health considerations, or is there something wrong?

I knew I'd have to stop some day. Why not now?

That was very nice, what you did for that couple just now. Breaking the rules to change their flight. Without nicotine you've become more charitable?

I wanted to see their faces light up. Did you notice when I said, about the fee, we're going to waive that? It was as if the room became brighter.

You see yourself as Edison? Or Dr. Phil?

I remembered a friend's story. How his parents were able to escape Nazi Germany because a Gestapo officer gave them forged papers. Really broke the rules. In my imagination, the official calls himself Schimmler, a compound of schlemiel and Himmler.

In your imagination, how would he know any Yiddish? From remarks of people he had saved? Referring to him as a schlemiel?

That's the point. He has a Jewish grandmother. She's Italian so they don't recognize the name. If it comes out, he's in the concentration camp.

The Gestapo doesn't recognize Italian Jewish names?

They've asked the Fascist secret police for a list, but all they got back was Ebraico. Not even Levi. They thought non-Aryan incompetence.

So perhaps Schimmler has a resistance-minded cousin in the Fascist secret police?

Could be a good plot device.

Then what happens?

Schimmler has an assistant from Hitler Youth. Lise. She's a complete Nazi brainwash and he's afraid she'll uncover the secret rescue of refugees and turn him in. Then they'll find his grandmother.

So he plots to have her eliminated?

He doesn't know what to do so he seduces her.

To have something on her?

Or to know more about her life, find out something. As a last resort, maybe murder her.

Of course she feels it's an honor to sleep with a Gestapo officer.

No, she's in love with him. She knows everything he's doing and thinks it's wonderful. The Hitler Youth façade is…

Just protective coloring, like Schimmler's Gestapo job.

In due course, Lise becomes pregnant. She will not raise a child in Nazi Germany so they come up with an escape scheme.

They forge papers for themselves!

Do you think it might sell?

Changing of nonrefundable discount tickets and waiving standard fees is in total disregard of airline rules. I'm going to report you.

Unless?

You seduce me. Now.

Carole locked the office door.

Nut Case

By Bob Burnett

I've heard about walking in your sleep, but I've never heard of writing stuff in your sleep.

I woke up this morning when the gates clanged open, sitting at my writing table with a pencil in my hand and this note in front of me. How could I write stuff using words I had to look up in the dictionary when I tried to read it? Words like "annihilated" and "motif."

Must have been one hell of a dream. Wish I could remember it. Or maybe I don't. I got enough trouble without this, what with them trying to say I'm a nut case. How could I write something like this? But it is my handwriting. So.

The only human we ever killed intentionally was Doctor Harold Slade. Doctor Slade was trying to destroy us. We do not regret his demise. He was a butcher who annihilated clusters by the trillions. Clan elders ignored our warnings. Our prophecy rebuffed without analysis, we were commanded to pursue proper growth motif, to divide as custom requires, and to leave clan functions to wiser clusters. They died for their arrogance. Our cluster is now senior-elder. We believe we have learned to communicate with our current host, and through him to explain events from our perspective. We do not intend harm. We would make peace. Please, accept our overtures and communicate with us.

Why would I write stuff like that? Dr. Slade is dead, but I didn't kill him. Complications from the flu, is what I heard.

I knew Doctor Slade from the nut ward in the prison hospital where they sent me for snatching out that con's eyeball. Did you know the thing that holds your eyeball in will stretch out like a rubber band before it pops and the eyeball comes off like a wet grape? Man, did that con holler!

I didn't kill Doctor Slade, so why would I confess to it? And why would I refer to myself as "we?" Last time I checked there was only one of me. I suppose if you read my rap-sheet you might think I was at least three people, but confessing to something you didn't do is for nut cases.

I'll bet if they found out I wrote something in my sleep I'd have to go back to the State Hospital and prove one more time that I'm not a nut case.

Maybe I should just burn that note.

Victor Charlie to Tower

By Heather Grange

"Don't stand too near the propellers," you say. We climb onto the wings, I feel lost in the small seat but a part of the wings and fuselage, we taxi, the noise is loud, the instrument panel looks complicated, then we have clearance. I am reliant on your expertise. I'm not thinking of mechanical or human failure.

Women are drawn to you. They sympathize over the loss of your wife who died in your arms and the young daughter you brought up alone. When I came along you had remarried and had two more girls. You are cultured and widely read, interested in Roman archaeology, wildlife and take aerial photos of crop marks, ancient buildings, castles in the snow and sailing ships at anchor. You hope to get them published one day. People stay loyal. You inspire confidence.

In those early days I volunteer to help in the office. The clubhouse is situated near a runway on the edge of a busy airport and noise is invasive. You are busy giving lessons in the Piper Cherokee or Cessna. Later, you take on instructors and new relationships are forged. Well-off, middle-aged women wander in and out, pose, flirt and extract the most from their first pre-flight briefings, solo, night flights and cross countries. They fall in love. It is true what they say about the flying world. There is no other like it. The more ambitious work towards the PPL and flying instructors and then First Officers.

At weekends the clubhouse is full. Everyone mixes: your family, weekend fliers, non-members who loll in armchairs and children who run around among the coffee cups and charts. Talk is of bowsers, Air Traffic Control, log books, RT, weather reports and long solo flights. Evening lectures and social gatherings are planned alongside celebrations for the first birthday party. Nominations go forward for the Pilot of the Year award. There are day trips. Do you remember being refused permission to take off at Ostend? You explained about the difference in daylight hours and we took off into the twilight. It is a time of coming and going.

I, too, move on. I marry in the Church at the end of the runway. In my wedding photo I am looking up listening to an aircraft taking off. My husband and I move abroad. On one of my trips home I come back to visit you. I didn't know it then but I won't see you again. I dream of you but each time my hand reaches out for yours, I wake up.

Many years later your book comes to me via a friend. There are seasonal pictures of woodlands, churches and villages taken in sunlight and moonlight. It is dedicated to 'all the people who have shared an aircraft with me.' I hear your voice, see your wrinkles, your grey hair, your camera and ordnance survey maps. You are smiling at me. Why now?

Circles

By T. Paul Buzan

The moon, liquid-brilliant, pours its silver luster into the night. Shadows cast by tall pines and burial mounds seem to move volitionally all along the mountain under this light. They chase one another like young animals at play.

There are stories that tell of those who long ago tended the warning beacons for which this mountain is named now wandering here after death – restless spirits waiting to be reborn.

On nights when the shadows rollick and dance the stories could be true.

It is late summer.

At dawn the sky still breaks against the mountain in waves of pale blue mist. The sun emerges and the waves of mist recede, drawn in to wait again for nightfall when once more they will lap against the mountain's face like the tides.

The clattering of my alarm clock shatters the sleep that surrounds me and I surface from a dream. I struggle to guard from marauding consciousness the fading apparition of a girl who is at once both as strange and remote to me as a fairy kingdom and the sum of every woman I've ever known, loved, cherished, cursed. Her ember eyes flash finally as the dream is outstripped by reality and I am left alone in the growing glow of morning.

In the kitchen my coffee maker exhales its resuscitating breath in periodic sighs. I pour a full cup. Ovid wrote of men who drank from the waters of Lethe in order to forget, to sleep eternally. I envy these men as I swallow a searing mouthful of coffee towards an opposite effect. But the drink is slow to act. My eyes remain heavy and with each blink a vague image of the girl I dreamt flits through my mind like one of the ghosts on the mountain.

I walk to the window.

Across from my apartment there is a small vegetable garden. Rows of pepper and bean plants, bellflowers with milky blossoms, and a pumpkin patch grow there. All are enclosed within the rusting links of a wire fence. Every day with bowed back and dirt covered knees the same old woman tends this garden. Standing at the window, the cup of coffee cooling in my hands, I watch her.

The old woman lays down her hand spade, straightens her back, inhales deeply and with knotted gnarled fingers begins turning over a pile of desiccated pepper plants beneath which grow seedlings their stems and leaves as pale with newness as the new day, seedlings protected and nourished through the decay and death of the plants from which their seeds were harvested, seedlings that in a short span of time will lay shriveled on the earth with new life burning under them and the old woman will strip the familiar shroud from their reincarnated selves as she has done since the time before her remembering and offer them anew to the creative chaos of the sun.

I finish the coffee and close my eyes. No image of the girl returns.

Poetry

The Argument

By Brad M. Bucklin

I forced the cold air
through my teeth, it
billowed like fog.
I screamed, raged
and hurled snowballs.
I stomped on puddles
and gobs of slush clung
to my boots like oatmeal;
the plopping sound infuriated me.
I went blind and stepped
away from myself long
enough to look back.
I saw that I was running
towards her.

My Wife is a Peculiar Bird

By Angel Zapata

At times, she is the ghost of a feather
caught in the mouth of a breeze.
Then, quite other times, she is the beak
pecking at the corners of my eyes.

Sometimes, she is a cloud soaring
shy and silver through a storm.
Just last night, a lank claw
nesting wicked in my hair.

Sometimes, greets me with a kiss,
the hint of an olive branch.
Moreover, a fury of wings
shotgunned to flight.

She is a peculiar bird uncaged,
a ripe apple drifting from a tree.
Mornings, quiet unfurling heat.
Evenings, a bed of ashen leaves.

She is a mirror reflecting bitter wind,
an angel dancing on the head of a pin.
Oh what strange love she brings,
like a coin wishing for a new fountain.

If Only I Could Appreciate the Irony

By Holly Day

I never thought this would be me
compulsively taking pregnancy tests
every time I feel sick

so hopeful

things were so much easier when I was younger
and took getting knocked up
for granted, like the first one
was so effortless
in such a wrong time

I never thought I end up like this
shouting for sex when my P.H. levels
were just right for conceiving, checking off
days on the calendar, fingers crossed
praying that we could come together just right
just one more time

in dog obedience class...

By John Yamrus

in dog obedience class...

for once,
my little Abby
did everything right.

for once,
she didn't
bite, jump or pull.

this time
she paid attention
and sat and stayed
and came
and listened...

just like all the other dogs.

i can't tell you how much
i hated that.

Meditation 37

By Anne Brooke

Cover my life
with angels.

Hammer them out
in gold
and place one
at my beginning
and one at my end.

Stretch their wings
wide over my days
so I may hide
within them.

Beached

By John Grey

A whale beached itself.
Some tried to heave it back into the water.
Others hung out in hopes to see it die.
And many just snapped picture after picture
to show the folks back home.

It was the whale that started the disagreement.
You said we should just leave it be,
that it was wrong to interfere with nature.
I argued that we interfere with nature
as a matter of course and are obliged,
when opportunity arises, to put things right.

Excuse the pun, but a whale of an argument ensued.
It soon left that poor stranded beast far behind,
encompassed, within its rage,
every difference of opinion, every trait we disliked in the other,
from the day we'd met.
Finally, we beached ourselves,
you in the bedroom, me on the couch.

But at three a.m., I, the one who advocated
taking action, said to myself, nothing doing.
And you, queen of leave-things-as-you-find-them,
came with hug and kisses to get me back to bed.
If only we had snapped our picture.

Gaze

By RD Armstrong

She pierces me with her stare:
two perfect
puddles of ink
I imagine I look like a deer
caught in the headlights
of a late-model destiny
Go on, then
hit me

About the Authors

Angel Zapata

Angel Zapata was born in NYC, but currently resides just outside of Augusta, Georgia. Some of his flash fiction and poetry has appeared or is forthcoming on Powder Burn Flash, Doorknobs & Bodypaint, Every Day Fiction, Every Day Poets, Membra Disjecta, Flashes in the Dark, and The Absent Willow Review. He is husband to his blond goddess and father of four boys obsessed with all things ninja. Visit his blog at: http://arageofangel.blogspot.com

Bob Burnett

Bob Burnett serves as resident computer nerd at an Iowa community action agency. Most of his writing is for technical manuals, but Bob's fiction has appeared in a half-dozen magazines (including the final issue of Potpourri) that folded after publishing his work, as well as several that survived that trauma. Great Western Fiction purchased a story, but folded before the story was printed. Bob refuses to accept responsibility for the demise of any of them. Currently, three of his stories may be seen on Rope and Wire and another on ElectricSpec Fiction (both of which are still functioning).

Anne Brooke

Bill Charles

Bill Charles is a native of New Orleans but left the city twenty years ago. He currently lives in Alabama and retired. When not playing golf or working around the house, He writes poems, short stories and essays, some of which have been published on line.

Brad M. Bucklin

Brad M. Bucklin received a Bachelor's Degree in English and Theatre from Windham College where he studied with John Irving. After moving to Los Angeles at 25, he worked as an actor for a number of years on such shows as "One Day At A Time," "Waverly Wonders," "Facts of Life," "Days of Our Lives" "Picket Fences" and in films that included "World War III," "Wavelength" "No Place to Hide" and more. He is a credited writer for "The Wedding Channel," and his stories have appeared in the "Brentwood Bla Bla," "Anemone," "Windham Free Press."

Caroline Burman

Caroline Burman is an aspiring writer/critic, living just outside of Charlotte, NC. Influences include Kurt Vonnegut, Hunter S. Thompson, Chuck Klosterman, Franz Kafka, The Simpsons, Larry David, etc. Will be attending Western Carolina University in the fall of 2009.

E.K. Entrada

E.K. Entrada work has appeared or is forthcoming in several print and online journals, including Monkeybicycle, Keyhole, Johnny America, Fiction Weekly, Kyoto Journal, Audience, and Every Day Fiction.

Elaine Medline

Elaine Medline is the author of the young adult novel That Silent Summer, published by Scholastic Canada in 1999. Elaine has also written two stories recently published in the online journal Salt River Review. She was previously a medical reporter for the Ottawa Citizen newspaper, and is now involved in health-care policy.

Grant J. Bergland

Grant J. Bergland is a high school film teacher and a graduate student in English Literature at Cal State East Bay. His parents met in a diner.

Heather Grange

Heather left school at 16, trained as a shorthand typist, became an Air Hostess, worked as a secretary in Paris for 16 years and was a mature student at university. Her poems have been published in the Imperial War Museum in London, small presses, two short stories broadcast by BBC Radio, fiction and articles published in newspapers and magazines.

Holly Day

Holly Day is a travel writing instructor living in Minneapolis, Minnesota, with her husband and two children. Her newest book is Walking Twin Cities.

Ian Lamberto

Ian Lamberto has been an avid writer for years, but has only recently decided to make the leap towards publication. He currently reside in Buffalo, NY, where, among the strong winds and mountains of snow, Ian is striving to complete a first novel.

James Bowler

James Bowler is twenty-five and living in Trenton. Ontario, Canada. He currently is pursuing a writing career, trying to get his name out there through prominent magazines. James has mostly written short stories in the genres of horror, suspense, sci-fi and adventure; but, has also dabbled in mystery and romance. He is also currently working on his first novel as well as a collaborative novel with a respected fellow author and friend.

James Cotter

James Cotter lives in Richmond, Virginia. He usually writes about health services research and aging, but every once in a while he ventures into fiction. He has two novels under review and a number of short stories. This story was inspired by a film by Ron Dyens. Some characters are strong in our minds from day one; others take a few re-writes to get correct. I think Harold will make it, but his eyes are definitely brown now.

John Ammirati

John Ammirati was born in Montgomery, Alabama in 1982. He currently lives in Manchester, England and sings for the band Amida.

John Bruce

John Bruce recently had a short story nominated for the 2008 Pushcart Prize. His writing has appeared recently, or will appear, in Backhand Stories, Cantaraville, The Cynic Online, Dark Sky Magazine, DOGZPLOT, Eskimo Pie, Hobson's Choice Zine, Holy Cuspidor, The Journal of Truth and Consequence, Literal Translations, Pear Noir!, Press 1, The Scruffy Dog Review, Word Riot, and Written Word. I have degrees in English from Dartmouth College and the University of Southern California.

John Grey

Australian born poet, US resident since late seventies. Works as financial systems analyst. Recently published in Slant, Briar Cliff Review and Albatross with work upcoming in Poetry East, Cape Rock and REAL.

John Wiswell

John Wiswell writes humor, horror, fantasy, science fiction, persona, satire, and sometimes an actual story. He maintains the Bathroom Monologues, a daily blog of micro-fiction, monologues and innovative prose at www.johnwiswell.blogspot.com. He has been published in Scifaikuest, the Lewisboro Ledger, Flashshot and Insidepulse.com.

John Yamrus

Since 1970 John Yamrus has published 2 novels and 15 volumes of poetry. More than 900 of his poems have appeared in magazines around the world. Selections of his work have been translated into several languages, most recently, Romanian.

Jordan Eudy

Leigh Byrne

Len Joy

Len Joy lives in Evanston, Illinois with his wife and three children. For fifteen years Joy owned and operated an automobile engine remanufacturing company with plants in Phoenix, Arizona, Richmond, Virginia and Willow Springs, Missouri. His work has appeared in Hobart, 3AM Magazine, NightsAndWeekends, GlassFire Magazine, Slow Trains, 21Stars Review, Boston Literary Magazine and The Daily Palette (Iowa Review).

A collection of his short fiction was published by Bannock Street Books earlier this year. An excerpt from his novel, "Desperado," will be published by Annalemma Magazine in the fall of 2009.

Michael McLaughlin

Patricia McCowan

Patricia McCowan's stories have appeared in the anthologies Dark Times, published by Ronsdale Press, and Cleavage: Breakaway Fiction for Real Girls, put out by Sumach Press. She has also had pieces published in both print and online versions of Maisonneuve Magazine. Her short story Reading the Field placed third in the

Eden Mills Writers' Festival and she was also invited to read at the Eden Mills Fringe with other up-and-coming writers. Patricia McCowan lives in Toronto.

RD Armstrong

Various pieces by RD Armstrong (Raindog) have appeared in Spillway, Pearl, Unwound, Haight Ashbury Review, Drinking With Bukowski, Art/Life, Genre, The Lummox Journal, bender, Pitchfork, Poetry Motel, Chiron Review, Momentum Magazine and others. His poems are anthologized in "Das Ist Alles," Pearl Editions 1995; "Last Call: A Legacy of Madness" (also editor), Vinegar Hill Press 1995; "Raising the Roof" (a fundraiser for Habitat For Humanity – Riverside, CA), 1998; "Maytag Heights" (a similar fundraiser for H4H – Long Beach, CA), Lummox Press 1999. He is the founder and editor of The Lummox Press, which publishes the Little Red Book (LRB) series (30+ titles and counting), the LRB Master series, The Lummox Journal (monthly small press/alternative "zine" digest now in it's 6th year), and several specialty-type publications.

He has published LRB for Linda Lerner, Gerald Locklin, Hugh Fox, Normal, Rick Smith, and many others. Smith's "The Wren Notebook" (published by Lummox Press in 2000) has been nominated for a Pen Center West (poetry) Book of the Year Award and was called "the best [small press] book of poetry in the year 2000 by Chiron reviewer, Tim Scannell. He has been twice nominated for a Pushcart Prize. Recent titles include: "Lost Highway" (Blues Poetry Anthology – 15 poets); "On/Off the Beaten Path" (a long road poem, the second); "Paper Heart Vol. 3 (Love poems); "A Journey Up the Coast" (the first road poem); "Eyes Like Mingus" (A Jazz Poetry Anthology – 12 poets). All are published by Lummox Press.

Richard Grossman

Richard Grossman is a retired scientist and has written a number of textbook chapters and edited fascinating volumes such as the Handbook of Vinyl Formulating (John Wiley) and The Mixing of Rubber (Chapman & Hall).

Ryan Sayles

Ryan Sayles was born and raised in Kansas City, MO. He spent seven years in the military in anti-terrorism and is now in law enforcement. He has a wife, son and daughter. And three tattoos.

Sarah R. Larson

Sarah R. Larson is a three-time winner of the Kaden Short Story award.

T. Paul Buzan

Originally from Kansas City, MO T. Paul Buzan has lived in Korea since August 2007. He has published in "10 Magazine" and at "ExPatLit.dotcom."

www.ingramcontent.com/pod-product-compliance
Lightning Source LLC
Chambersburg PA
CBHW020138180626
46810CB00004B/1625